My Boyfriend's Wife

A novel

Mychea

Good 2 Go Publishing

Published by:
GOOD2GO PUBLISHING
7311 W. Glass Lane
Laveen, AZ 85339
www.good2gopublishing.com
Twitter @good2gobooks
G2G@good2gopublishing.com
Facebook.com/good2gopublishing
ThirdLane Marketing: Brian James
Brian@good2gopublishing.com

Cover design: Davida Baldwin
ISBN: 978-0989185974

Books by This Author

Coveted
Vengeance
He Loves Me, He Loves You Not
He Loves Me, He Loves You Not 2 Puppetmaster
My Boyfriend's Wife

Acknowledgments

Crystal Hall, "my everything" (lol) Thank you for being you. For long road trips to book signings, taking time out of your life to invest in #teammychea! You rock and are truly invaluable to me beyond measure. I appreciate you from the bottom of my heart. Let's get it!! Whoop whoop!!

Cee thank you for being such a loyal fan supporting me at The Literary Book Joint, you definitely rock girl!! Much appreciated!

Can't not shout out my hometown bookstore The Literary Joint who continually let me come and do my thing there. Much love to Quita and Shaun always!!!

Thank you to my amazing editor Valdenia Simmons for helping to make my story so much better! Much appreciated!

Thanks to Silk White for the continual belief in my talent.

To my amazing fans, you all are the absolute best! Thank you so much for being faithful readers of my crazy, twisted tales and for rocking out with me each time. I love you all.

Okay, get ready....it's time to let the drama begin! Enjoy!

Prelude

The water dripped at a slow steady pace from the kitchen faucet into the deep sterling silver sink. The curtains blew outward in a silken wave as air passed through the window sitting ajar, allowing the cool spring air to drift in. Crickets continued singing their evening lullaby into the still night as sirens wailing in the distance moves in urgency toward their destination.

Opening tired eyes as she glanced at the digital clock on her deep cherry wood nightstand that reflected 2:30 AM back at her, Ananda sighed in frustration as she realized that tonight would be another restless night. She hadn't been able to sleep since she'd found out the news that had changed her world as she knew it to be forever. Taking a deep sigh as she shifted onto her side, she pulled her down comforter over her head and closed her heavy eyelids praying for peace.

The sudden, shrill ringing of the phone caused Ananda to give up any notion of resting for the night. Throwing the comforter off of her body instantly caused her to shiver in the cool room. She rose from the bed to retrieve her cell phone from her black Michael Kors purse that sat on the floor by the doorway to her bedroom.

"Hey." Ananda said into the phone as she lay back down across her king size memory foam bed.

"Girl, what you doing?"

"I was lying down trying to sleep like normal people do. It's like 2:45 in the morning." Ananda replied sarcastically, mood worsening by the minute.

"Don't bite my head off. I just wanted to check on you." The caller responded indignantly.

"I'm sorry Tracey." Ananda said immediately regretting snapping at her. "I'm just going through a lot right now."

"I know you are." Tracey said softening her tone. "I figured you were probably up. That's why I called you this late."

"Thank you. I really appreciate it. Just having a hard time dealing you know?"

"Yeah." Tracey spoke in sympathy. "I can only imagine."

"It's like I keep replaying it over and over in my mind trying to figure out what happened. What I did wrong. How could I have stopped the situation from happening?" Ananda swallowed audibly trying to hold off the tears, "You know Tray. What did I do to deserve something like this to happen to me?"

"You didn't do anything. No one deserves to have anything of this magnitude to happen to them." Tracey's words offered little solace.

"I mean, I know I'm not exempt from anything, but how much is a woman supposed to take? I mean damn!" Ananda was angry, hurt and frustrated. She wanted to kill someone, bash something; anything that would make her feel better or at the very least allow her to get back the last three years of her life. "I'm sorry Tray, let me call you later. I'm just not in the mood to talk right now." Ananda said as she hung up not waiting for Tracey's response.

Leaning over the side of her bed, Ananda pulled her Ed Hardy journal from underneath of it and begin to write.

August 24, 2013

Yeah, they sit behind their "perfect" bubble gum world and talk about me; judging me, but I could give two shits. They don't know me or what I represent. I didn't know I was the other woman. In my world I was his woman. That's what he told me, that's what I believed; or is that what I wanted to believe? Either way, why she hating me? I'm not the one that lied to her or cheated. If anything I should hate her, she's living my life the one I should have had. Why waste energy hating me? I want to ask her. He comes home to you every night, where y'all are the one's making memories and taking family portraits. I spend holidays alone; no birthdays celebrated. She gets to have that...a real life;

my life, but do I hate her? No. That's the difference between me and her. He ruined my life not hers. He made me think we were going to be forever, not her. He made me love him knowing he was living a double life, not her. But she keeps testing me and the angel on my right and the devil on my left are having conflicting thoughts...both can't win, so for her safety and my sanity I really hope she learns to value her life and leave me to mine.

A knock at the front door halted Ananda's pen. It was now three in the morning and she had no idea who would be coming to see her at this late hour. Putting the journal back under her bed she walked to the door and looked through the peephole. Shocked she opened the door to stare at the person responsible for her hurt.

****

There she sat in the middle of the new hardwood floor she'd recently had installed with her legs folded beneath her body. Smoke billowing about her as she dragged one long puff after another off of her Newport cigarette into her air deprived lungs she sat in the foyer, eyes glued to the front door willing her husband to come home. Encased in darkness, the reddish spark from her slender white nicotine addiction was the only thing illuminating the eerily still house as the clock struck three a.m. Her ears were being serenaded by the sound of Etta James singing *All I Could Do Was Cry* from the iPad he'd bought her as a birthday present the previous year. She listened as the words of the song etched themselves into her soul, "All I could do, all I could do was cry. All I could do was cry, I was losing the man that I loved, and all I could do was cry."

A year ago her tears would have made a steady rhythmic descent down her face, but not now. Now, at this moment in time she has decided that she has dealt with more than her fair share of heartache and now she would make sure that he will deal with the consequences of his actions! She knew that most people believed in letting karma handle their problems for them, but her time and her patience was short and karma will take far too long. She was going to see to it that everything happens as it should if it was the last thing that she was to do on this earth. She would make him see without a doubt that she would always be his one and only, "till death do us part."

My Boyfriend's Wife

As tears become rivers emptying into a sea of pain,
there you'll find my heart, smashed into a thousand pieces littered in
the rain.
Amongst the shadows is where you'll see
a glimpse of the woman I used to be.
I used to believe in the good of everything, everyone;
an optimist...nothing could cloud my day; my world
I met him on a sunny June day and knew he was heaven sent
the sun shined brighter, the world was happier;
here standing in front of me was the one
I'd waited my whole life for
Him, my destroyer, the man that cracked my universe
and taught me things and people weren't always what they seemed
and no matter how I tried, there was no longer a sun in sight to see
I trusted him, gave my heart to him; he used me; did he ever love
me?
Does he know what love means? Loyalty? Please!
He has none, except to himself...
I lost myself in him and his world; who am I? I'm not sure
They call me Ananda, I call me damaged
I'm not who I used to be and unsure of who I'm supposed to be
and there is the problem...
I'm a broken reflection of someone I used to know and can never be
again
am I better or worse after him?
My heart is definitely worse,
but my spirit--the one thing he couldn't touch is unbroken
my spirit survived his wrath
and in due time
so will I....

Mychea

The end is near....

She stared at the two of them lost in their own little world, oblivious to any and everything besides each other. Consumed in a world that she could never be a part of and totally unconscious to the imminent threat was lurking nearby. In this world --or the next-- he was going to belong to her. The weight of her heart seemed to match the weight of the weapon in her hand. There would be hell to pay. She was going to see to it.

~ His one and only, till death do they part

One

Christmas Eve 2007

*T*hanks to a teenage girl, whose headphone volume had to be dialed up to the highest notch it could go, Mariah Carey's 'All I want for Christmas' serenaded everyone on the rush hour train leading from the city into the suburbs. A frustrated Ananda ran her fingers through her short curly hair as a woman pushing her baby in a stroller rolled over her foot for the fifth time in less than two minutes. She was standing in the middle of the aisle on the Orange Line train holding onto the bar above her headed toward her stop at New Carrollton Station, which as far she was concerned, couldn't come soon enough.

"Hello." Ananda yelled into her phone after feeling it vibrate in her hand.

"What you doing?" Her friend Tracey asked her.

"What Tray? I can barely hear you." Ananda said before her signal died on her cell. Tracey knew that she was on the train. She called at the same time everyday expecting a different result. Ananda chuckled quietly to herself at her crazy friend and prayed for her stop to come a little faster.

Ten minutes later Ananda was in her car Skeeter headed home; she loved her some Skeeter. Skeeter was a 1998 green Buick Regal and they had been through a lot together. Ananda was riding with the windows down because it felt like it was100 degrees outside confirming what she had been long telling her friends, that the world was soon coming to an end. There was no reason it should be this hot in the state of Maryland in December and on top of that Skeeter's air had been broken for the last two years. Ananda wanted to fix her, but funds were tight and she was barely making it as it was. Fixing the air conditioning in her car was the least of her worries when she was more concerned with keeping the lights on in her apartment. But in spite of it all, Christmas was her favorite time of the year and even though she was tired she was anxious to get home to wrap the remaining gifts she had for her family and boyfriend.

Waiting at the light on Route 450, Ananda tilted her head back onto the headrest and closed her eyes as the heat threatened to smother her. She couldn't wait to get home on the other side of town across the bridge in Alexandria, Virginia, but she had told her mother that she would stop by for a few minutes. Her mother had made some of her amazing chicken salad and had set aside a portion for her to take home and by no means could she pass up on such a treat.

"Hey Ma!" Ananda yelled as she walked into the unlocked door of her mother's condo. As usual, she had it unlocked and waiting for her after she'd heard her pull up.

"Hey boo. Did you have your music loud enough? I heard you get off the highway and start heading this way five minutes ago." Ananda shook her head smiling as she gave her mom a kiss on the cheek and went to wash her hands in the sink. This woman could find an excuse to fuss about any and everything, if you say the moon is shining she would say it could be brighter if a cloud wasn't blocking it.

"You know I like to get my party on in my ride." Ananda laughed as she picked up a spoon from the counter and reached for the big bowl of chicken salad sitting on the table.

Her mom smacked her arm lightly, "Girl I know if you don't get that spoon away from my bowl there's going to be problems. Yours is in the fridge."

"Why can't I have some of this one?" Ananda asked in mock indignation.

"Because I said so, now get yours and leave this one alone." Ananda placed the spoon back on the table.

"Yes ma'am." As soon as her mother turned her back she grabbed the spoon and snuck a small spoon full into her mouth and then headed toward the dining room.

"Your mail is on the table in there." Her mother yelled from the kitchen, "and I saw you get some chicken salad, you not slick. Don't you touch it **again**" she warned.

Ananda burst into laughter as she chewed what was left in her mouth and retrieved her mail off the table. One of these days, she was really going to have to forward her mail to her apartment.

"Okay Ma, I'm out. I'm tired and I still have to drive across town. Christmas is tomorrow, don't forget." Ananda teased.

"Right, like you would allow me to forget. See you tomorrow." Her mother yelled out after her.

Back in Skeeter Ananda was anxious for some chill time. She made it home in record time. Upon entering the serenity of her apartment, Ananda left her shoes and purse at the door and immediately plugged in the lights that brought her Christmas tree to life. Flopping onto her chenille chocolate sofa to relax for a moment Ananda glanced at the Rolex sitting on her coffee table that she had splurged over nineteen hundred dollars to buy for her boyfriend Braxton. He loved watches and this year she wanted to do something really nice for him, especially since she anticipated him doing something special for her in return. She'd started saving since last Christmas and even though it wasn't the most expensive Rolex out there, it was *still* a Rolex and she knew that he would be excited about it. Leaning her head back onto the cushions Ananda promptly felt her eyes begin to close. She had to admit that she was tired as she decided to give in to a wave of sleepiness coming over her.

A few moments later her ringing cell phone jarred her out of her light slumber. Standing slowly and starting toward her purse, she felt as if someone had drugged her. Seeing Braxton's name flash across her screen seemed to reenergize her and Ananda's mood picked up a little as well. She loved her delicious man. They had been dating for two years and she just knew that any day now he would be proposing.

"Hey babe. You felt me missing you?" She purred into the receiver.

"Nah not really. Hey I gotta talk to you for a minute."

Ananda was taken aback by his brashness. "I mean. Don't mind my feelings any. Geez. What's going on?" She asked with an attitude. Just that fast Braxton had irritated her after she had been so happy to hear from him.

"It's not you, it's me." He began.

"Huh?" Ananda was confused, "What are you talking about? What do you mean? It's not me it's you, wha===?"

"Me, you, us." he said stopping her, "This thing we got going is not working for me."

Ananda narrowed her eyes in disbelief at the phone in her hand as Braxton uttered those words to her. "Seriously? After all this time together that's the best you can do?" Voice laced with enough venom to kill him with the mere bite of her words she continued, "You don't feel like you owe me just a little more than that?"

"What you mean?" Braxton asked innocently as if he couldn't comprehend Ananda's issue.

"You're so full of it." Ananda's annoyed voice rose dramatically on her side of the phone. "You don't even have the decency to tell me face to face. This is a punk ass move right here."

"I'm saying, what do you mean?"

Ananda didn't hear the rest of Braxton's statement because she pressed the End button on him and threw the phone onto the sofa. *The nerve.* She thought to herself. This was supposed to be the year he proposed to her. This was supposed to be her moment and he had ruined it. Seeing the sleek stainless steel Rolex on the table Ananda's mood promptly worsened. Running to the table and snatching up the watch she wondered what she had been thinking spending so much on a piece of steel for an ungrateful piece of a man. He didn't care enough about her to let her know to her face that he was no longer interested in their relationship. *Two years!* She began thinking about all of the time she would never get back. Her hurt soon morphed into red-hot anger. *And at Christmas!! He is just a cheap, lying, low-life dog.* She wondered if the Rolex was returnable, if not she would get right on Craig's List or Ebay and take the best offer from anyone interested in having a brand new Rolex. Either way she was going to get her money back.

Pacing around the living room, she glanced around and noticed for the first time that there were more photos of her and Braxton than there were of her alone or with anyone else she went into a fit of rage. Ananda stomped over to the photos and knocked them all off of their prospective perches, giving a satisfied grin when she heard them hit the floor as glass begin to shatter everywhere from the frames.

Once every frame lay in a mangled mess of broken glass, twisted metal and shattered wood on the floor, Ananda walked to the hall bathroom to retrieve a waste basket. While bending down to clean up the damage that she had caused her eyes locked onto one of her favorite pictures of she and Braxton that had previously sat on her coffee table. As Ananda reached to pick up the photo, in a cruel stroke of irony, a piece of glass sliced through her ring finger, causing it to bleed. She gently suckled on her injured finger and used her other hand to retrieve the photo from the mess on the floor, more carefully this time to avoid the broken glass. Ananda stared at their animated faces as she continued sucking on her finger, observing how she and Braxton had joyfully smiled at the camera man who had taken their photo at the entry gate to Kings Dominion.

Braxton had been ultra sexy that day baring a striking resemblance to Laz Alonzo in the photo. His sunglasses shielding the honey brown eyes she so loved to love to gaze into. Her face crumpling up in disgust, she threw the picture into the wastebasket and commenced cleaning up the disaster she had created in her living room. She refused to waste one more minute of her time focused on Braxton when she knew for certain that he wasn't focused on her.

An hour later Ananda stood back and admired her work. Her place was back in order and completely devoid of any photos that included Braxton. She was happy to be done with it. She wasn't the type of woman to cry over a man, she had been there and done that earlier on in her life. At twenty-eight she could do without all the dramatics. If a man didn't want to be a part of her life, she could live with that. Let him keep it moving. She wasn't in the business of keeping a man that didn't want to be kept. Returning the wastebasket to its place in the bathroom she ran back to the living room when she heard her cell ringing again and prayed to God that it wasn't Braxton hitting her back up. Seeing Tracey flash across her screen Ananda relaxed. "Hey Tray." She answered.

"You didn't call me back. What are you doing?"

Ananda smiled in spite of herself at the sound of Tracey's anxious voice. "Just finished throwing away some garbage, what are you up too?" Ananda asked her as she sat down in her matching chocolate chair that sitting adjacent to her sofa.

"Girl, I am down here at the stadium. You will never guess who showed up with some raunchy ghetto chick on his arm."

"Who?" Ananda asked in a bored uninterested tone. Tracey was always seeing some foolishness that she felt like she just had to share, so this was nothing new.

"Braxton! Your Braxton, girl! Slobbing down this nasty hoe in public and everything! If you want me to I can get close up behind her and punch her in her neck." Tracey's voice got low like she was sneaking up on the woman already.

"Oh, that's it?"

"What you mean that's it?" Tracey responded in a shocked tone, "Ana he doing everything but bumping and grinding this chick. And you know I don't play that, no ma'am. If you need me to handle this for you, I got you."

Ananda closed her eyes and sighed, "Braxton is no longer my concern, so don't waste your energy. Forget about him."

"Since when?" Tracey asked in disbelief, "Just last weekend you had me at the mall in every jewelry store trying on potential engagement rings. Now all of a sudden he is no longer your concern? So what happened? Are you okay? Spill it, because I need to hear this one."

Ananda curled her feet up under her in the chair and closed her eyes. She wasn't really in the mood to recap her conversation with Braxton, but she knew Tracey wasn't going to let up without an explanation.

"Since you must know, he gave me the whole it's not you, it's me story, with his selfish ass."

"You lying! No he didn't." Tracey exclaimed, "Girl these men out here these days are something else." There was a pregnant pause before Tracey spoke again. "Ok, so what's the plan? We slashing tires, breaking windshields, getting his utilities cut off? What?"

Ananda began to laugh. Leave it to Tracey to try and start a personal war.

"No girl! We are not doing any of that."

"You sure? Because I'm right here. I can go straight to his car and tear some stuff up!"

Ananda smiled and shook her head loving Tracey's loyalty. "Seriously Tray, leave it alone. Don't go doing anything crazy. I'm done with it and you should be too." Ananda's voice carried the weight of finality.

"Ok, I won't say another word. Just let me say this one thing real quick."

"I thought you weren't going to say another word?" A bemused Ananda interjected.

"Yeah, you right. I'll keep it to myself."

"Good. Enjoy your night. I'm going to lie down. My head is suddenly pounding."

"Okay, lie down and get some sleep. I'm here if you change your mind about anything I suggested."

"I know you are Tray. Love you."

"Love you." Ananda heard her respond before ending the call.

****

Christmas Day 2007

Lazily watching the white snow fall like cotton outside the hospital window, Malcolm sat in the dimly lit room holding a sleeping brown bundle in his arms. His heart was completely full and he had nothing but a mountain of love to give on this day that he had received the most precious gift that the world could give. Breaking his trance from the peaceful snowfall Malcolm gazed down into the tiny face that appeared to be in a heavenly slumber. He never imagined that he would feel like this. This is my daughter I'm holding in my arms he thought.

"I know, it's crazy right?" Merci said gazing at him as she lay in the hospital bed while her nurse checked on her and made a few notations on the clipboard. "We brought this little person in the world."

"I know." Malcolm's voice was choked with emotion. He hadn't thought that his and Merci's relationship would survive past the first month let alone the length of a pregnancy, but here they are, seven years in and new parents to a beautiful baby girl. "It *is* crazy" he said. Merci had been his girl since he was eighteen. She was cute, a little on the thick side, borderline chunky but he liked his women with meat on their bones. She had held him down for the past seven years of his life, when things with his folks hadn't been working out and he'd needed to find his purpose in life. He owed the world to her and would do just about anything for her. The only problem was she got on his nerves. Her attitude constantly pushed him to the edge and if she hadn't gotten pregnant he would have left her already and -- he knew that she knew it.

Merci gazed at Malcolm's curly black hair and milk chocolate skin as he held their new daughter in his arms, satisfied with the turn of events. She knew that she now had Malcolm right where she he needed him to be. He was so elated about his new title as father to their *miracle* baby that he wasn't too focused on how this wonderful miracle came to be and Merci was prepared to take the secret to her grave. From the beginning, he made a big deal about not wanting any children -- ever. So she told Malcolm that she was sterile and couldn't have any more children after her daughter Tatiana who was only an infant when they'd first began dating. As she continued staring at the two, Merci smiled. Malcolm would be hers forever now.

Laying her head of long braided locks deep into the plush pillows that the nurse had fluffed for her Merci closed her eyes for a nap. It had only been two hours since she'd given birth to their daughter Caprice and she was exhausted.

Malcolm looked over at the bed when he heard Merci's slow steady breathing, happy that she had finally gone to sleep. He had done his job and made sure she carried their baby to term with no problems. Now that his princess was here, things were going to change. He was going to do his best to make things work with Merci, but he wasn't about to be playing games with her either.

Things with them hadn't been all bad. He remembered good times with Merci. Back in the day when he'd been trying to sort himself out; Merci was the best thing for him. He was just a kid and Merci was six years his senior, even though most of the time you couldn't tell it. He would always be grateful for her but it was time for them to part ways. He was a businessman now and prided himself on not becoming another black male statistic by making something of himself. He knew Merci thought she had thrown a monkey wrench into his life by getting pregnant and using the situation to hold on to him. He hadn't bought that whole sterile story when they first met, but times had been hard and he had to do what he had to do and Merci was what he needed at the time. She had been doing her thing and taking care of her newborn daughter Tatiana and handling her business. He always respected a hustler in any capacity that they came and Merci had been on her grind. But somewhere along the line, she had gotten spoiled and now she expected the world out of Malcolm. At one point, he thought that he wanted to marry her and had even proposed to her. But the constant bickering and her trust issues caused him to break up the engagement to allow more time to get to know one another. Now after seven years he was positive that she wasn't the woman that he needed in his life anymore.

"You're deep in thought. Want to talk about it?" Startled by her voice, Malcolm looked over at Merci surprised to see her awake, unaware that he had been lost in his thoughts for so long.

"No, I'm okay." He responded glancing down at Caprice as she began moving around in his arms. Merci raised herself up in the bed a little.

"Bring her to me. She's getting hungry." Merci held her arms out to receive Caprice as Malcolm handed their daughter to her. Sitting back in the uncomfortable hospital chair, he watched as Merci nursed Caprice and was pleasantly surprised as how much he enjoyed listening to his new daughter as she ate. Yet he was in turmoil. He had to figure out a way to be a great father to his daughter without being Merci's "*man.*" And he could only imagine the problems that were going to surface as a result.

Two

$\mathcal{H}$unter Lewis sat on the beach enjoying the view of the many beautiful women walking around topless. This was one of the main reasons why he has enjoyed Florida's Haulover Beach located just north of South Beach. Sporting a pair of aqua beach shorts that matched the water, stretched out in a lounge chair that his assistant Lorna had arranged for him, Hunter knew that he was supposed to be enjoying his vacation. But he couldn't do that without allowing himself to get a little work done as well. After all he didn't become CEO of Lyrehc Entertainment Management being lazy or wasting precious time taking vacations. Work is not only what he loved to do, but he seemed to thrive from it. At two years old his company was relatively new, but he was on a mission to become a multi-millionaire even if it killed him. But in order to do that he had to live the lifestyle of the people who could afford him that opportunity. This is why he had decided to take this *working* vacation along with many of the CEO's from various Fortune 500 companies at this networking convention in Miami. He wasn't included on the invite list this time around but he was making it a point to meet enough people and become enough of a factor to ensure that he makes that exclusive guest list next year.

"Mr. Lewis. I was able to pull a few strings and get you into an event for this evening."

Lowering his laptop Hunter sat up in his lounge chair giving Lorna his undivided attention. "Were you now? What event is that?" he asked while taking in her appearance. Lorna was an attractive brunette with a striking resemblance to Scarlett Johansson. More than once Hunter had toyed with the thought of a fling with her, but she was exceptional at her job and he never mixed business with pleasure. The idea of having to go through the pains of replacing her with someone new for nothing more than a meaningless dalliance with Lorna made his stomach cringe.

"It is an informational event for all the top marketing organizations" she said as she proudly handed him two VIP tickets.

Glancing down at the tickets that had been placed in his hand, Hunter read the title *Managing the Next "Big It" Celebrity. What Every Manager in Today's Entertainment Needs to Know.*

"Is this a seminar?" Hunter asked raising his light brown eyes up to meet Lorna's dark drown ones.

Lorna tipped her head to the side taking in her undeniably sexy boss. "More like a networking dinner I was told. There will be two keynote speakers that will speak for thirty minutes each. The next three hours of the event are for you to schmooze it up with other executives and to make business connections that will hopefully turn into investors and other potential partnerships."

"I see." Hunter replied as he shifted the tickets in his hand, "and I needed two tickets?" he asks in mock puzzlement.

Lorna gave him a stunning smile, "You'll need a date of course and I'm available providing that my boss gives me the evening off."

Hunter smiled. He knew Lorna had a crush on him and momentarily allowed a brief thought about getting it on with her but quickly remembered mantra that business always comes before pleasure. "You can go, but you will not have the evening off. This is a working event and I need you to be my eyes and ears." Hunter gave Lorna a stern stare, "Okay?"

"Absolutely! I am the epitome of professionalism."

"Yes you are. Thank you for being that way." Hunter stood to his feet. "I'm going back to the room to take a nap and get ready for this evening. We will meet in the lobby at 7:30 sharp." Hunter looked down in Lorna's eyes, "Does that sound good to you?"

"Sounds perfect. I'll arrange a car for us and see you then."

"Great." Hunter said as he headed back towards the W where he and Lorna were staying in the E-Wow Suite. He couldn't deny, at $5,100 a night the experience was very pleasant and worth every dime.

Later that evening Lorna was sitting in the lobby waiting on Mr. Lewis to appear for their evening out. Even though they were sharing a suite together, she rarely saw him. She knew he made it a point to be scarce whenever they were in such confined quarters.

"Ready?" Lorna's head turned swiftly to the side when she heard his deep alluring voice. She turned and her eyes found him standing there, dark chocolate, 6 foot1, dressed in a black suit, with an electric blue shirt-- Lorna literally felt her mouth drop open. Certainly she was used to Mr. Lewis dressing nicely, but tonight he simply took her breath away. If one didn't look closely he could easily be mistaken for Lance Gross. Lorna had to admit that Mr. Lewis was looking especially snazzy tonight.

As Lorna stood dumbstruck Hunter took in her appearance as well. She was dressed to kill in a classy silk evening gown. He hated to admit it, but she looked good enough to eat. And Lorna knew that she looked good. She could see the appreciation in Mr. Lewis' eyes. She was clothed in a shiny silk lace dress with a nude underlay. The dress had a keyhole opening in the front and back that accentuated her slim back, narrow waist and D cup breasts and then draped to the floor with a front slit.

"You look amazing." Hunter told Lorna as he extended his arm out to her.

"Thank you. You're not too shabby yourself" she told him. She took his extended arm and he escorted her out the glass doors of the hotel lobby to their waiting town car.

When the two of them arrived at the beach where the event was being held, they were checked in and then instructed to remove their shoes and follow the red carpet down towards the water where the tents were located.

"This is interesting." Lorna remarked as she lifted her dress so it wouldn't drag in the sand and held onto Hunter's arm with her other hand.

"Very." Hunter replied as he took in the area where everyone had gathered to hear the first speaker. He and Lorna were late and there was nothing Hunter hated more than being late for an event.

"Let's go." Hunter snapped as he abruptly turned and led them back the way they had just recently come.

"What's wrong?" Lorna asked almost falling in the sand as she tried to keep up with the pace of his stride. She knew that he was angry, but it wasn't her fault. She had made sure they got here promptly at 8:00.

"You know I cannot tolerate being tardy to an event. It is unprofessional and makes me look ridiculous." Hunter was boiling on the inside, part of him had a mind to leave Lorna there and make her figure out how to get back, but even he wasn't that much of an ass to leave her out here to fend for herself.

Lorna opted not to say anything as they waited for the valet to pull their car around. When Mr. Lewis was in one of his moods like this it was wise to fade into the background. When they arrived back at the hotel, Hunter respectfully opened the car door for Lorna and then watched as she went into the hotel. Getting back into the car Hunter headed to the popular Mangos bar to have a drink and watch the ladies dance around in their festive costumes as he tried to blow off some steam.

Making it back to the suite around four in the morning Hunter was stinky drunk. Stumbling around the suite as he searched for the light switch he dropped his key when he ran into a coffee table and knocked the glass lamp to the floor.

Awakened by the commotion, Lorna leapt out of bed clad only in black lace panties and topless. She tended to get hot when she slept so she chose to sleep in next to nothing. Running into the living room to see what all the commotion was about, she flipped on a light switch and found Hunter in a discombobulated heap on the floor.

"Oh no! Mr. Lewis, are you alright?"

Hunter heard a voice speaking to him and when he opened his eyes he saw a beautiful angel. Through his drunken haze, it appeared that a bright light framed her body and he wondered if he had somehow died and was in heaven. He smiled at her thinking that heaven was going to be a wonderful place if his arrival committee was any indication of things to come.

"They sent you to guide me into the pearly gates? I am indeed a lucky man." He mumbled before shutting his eyes again.

Lorna caught a whiff of Hunter's breath and surmised that he was definitely drunk out of his mind.

"Mr. Lewis, I think you've had a bit much to drink." Lorna reached down grabbing his arms attempting to help him to his feet. "Let me help you to bed."

"Will you join me?" Hunter asked as he pulled his enchanted angel into his arms. She smelled like a freshly picked strawberry, he had no idea that angels could smell so sweet. "Do you taste as good as you smell?" He asked her and before she could answer, he leaned down to see for himself.

Lorna melted into Hunter's kiss, she knew that she was taking advantage of the situation but she didn't care. There would never be another opportunity that Hunter would allow her to be this close to him and touching her the way that he was. She would worry about the consequences in the morning, for now she welcomed his advances. When he deepened the kiss moving his hands to her black lace panties and hooked his finger under the elastic as he gently pulled them down Lorna thought it would be rude to stop him. After all she believed in being an exemplary employee and she was going to give him a night he'd wish that he could remember.

$\mathcal{T}hree$

$\mathcal{I}$ love this man with all of my heart, she thought as she walked

down the aisle to meet him at the front next to the minister. She was smiling at him so hard that her cheekbones were beginning to hurt and she didn't care.

He was gazing at her with a soft smile that didn't quite reach his eyes and she knew his heart wasn't in it as hers was, but she didn't care. She could love enough for the both of them. She knew that she could. Come heaven or earth she was going to make this marriage work if it killed her.

Watching as he professed his love to her through sickness and health, to love and cherish her till death they did part. She knew deep down that he didn't mean it. She knew that he loved her, she just wasn't sure about the till death do they part component of it. She knew his decision to get married was to offset the chaos in his life, but she was going to milk this for what it was worth and he wasn't going anywhere as long as breath still pushed through her lungs and blood ran through her veins.

Four

June 15, 2010

Feeling she was getting too comfortable on the sofa Ananda

stood and headed to her bedroom to lie on her bed. No sooner had she closed her eyes did she hear her front door open and close.

"Ana! Where are you?"

Ananda let out a low groan regretting that she had given Tracey a key to her apartment.

"Here you are. You look like death warmed over." Tracey stood at her bedroom doorway eyeballing her.

"Gee thanks." Ananda responded opening one eye to see what Tracey was up to, "What's up?"

"How do you feel about going out tonight?" Tracey asked her. "Cameron has been sitting on my last nerve and I need some kind of release before I take his head off."

Taking in Tracey's ferocious expression as she gazed at herself in the mirror hanging over the dresser Ananda knew that she was going to lose the battle of staying in tonight. She was exhausted because her job has drained her in every sense of the word. Having to sit in an office all day everyday wasn't what she wanted to do with her life and she hated it. Ananda knew that Tracey tended to stress out over her relationship with Cameron and that she probably could use some sort of distraction from her situation, but she really wasn't in the mood to help her friend out in this way, at least not tonight.

Peering through one eye, Ananda continued to lie among her fluffy pillows detesting the very thought of abandoning her lusciously comfortable bed to go out with Tracey, but she told herself that's what friends are for.

"What do you have in mind?" Ananda raised one of her arms above her head, before continuing, "Please don't say a club, my headache is on a hundred. I don't think I can take all that loud music and chaos tonight."

"What about Busboys and Poets? It's Tuesday and they usually do spoken word in the evenings."

Ananda opened her tired red rimmed eyes to stare into Tracey's big, brown hopeful one's. "Okay. I'm only going because I love you." she sighed as she attempted to push her weary body off the bed.

Tracey's smile instantly brightened up her face, so much so that Ananda couldn't help but smile back at her and her cuteness. Tracey was standing in front of the mirror resembling a young Cree Summer when she played Freddie on a Different World. She had the same crinkly hair and there was an earthiness that radiated from her.

"Okay, okay. Give me about thirty minutes and then we can head out." Ananda told her as she finally was able to pull herself off the bed and stroll into her walk-in closet.

Roughly an hour later they walked into the Busboys and Poets on 14th street in downtown D.C. while a woman was doing a segment on the trials she endured while incarcerated. Listening to her story as the host guided them toward a table in the back, Ananda couldn't imagine what it would be like if she had to do prison time. She was thankful that her mother had done her best to steer her in a better direction when her attitude tended to get the best of her and led her to numerous fights during her teenage years. She had done one night in jail at the age of sixteen and was effectively scared straight, declaring never to go back again; so far she had held true to that vow.

Tracey picked up the menu and began flipping through it once they were seated, "I am starving."

Ananda smirked at her. "Hungry much?" She laughed.

Tracey's face cracked into a smile. "Whatever. I definitely gets my eat on."

"Mmmmhmm, you need to slow down." Ananda said giving her the once over from head to toe.

Tracey's eyes widened and her mouth dropped open in horror. "Are you saying I'm getting fat?"

"I would never say anything like that to you ever, but I think Cam is stressing you out and you're looking to food as an anesthetic." Ananda told her honestly.

Immediately Tracey put the menu down. "Cameron is stressing me out." she agreed, "I don't know what to do about him."

The waiter came to the table bringing them water and to inquire about their food choices. Once they gave the waiter their order Ananda leaned in close to Tracey.

"What is it that Cam has been doing?"

"What isn't he doing would be an easier question to answer."

Ananda took in Tracey's forlorn expression and really didn't know what to do or say to her friend. The look Tracey had on her face is precisely the reason why Ananda chose to stay single. She enjoyed her life drama free. She thought about all the past fights she had been in due to men and the whole Braxton fiasco years early left her pleasantly happy to be alone.

"Speaking of the devil, that's Cameron's calling now." Tracey said with a sigh as her phone vibrated at the table. "I'll be right back." She got up from the table and headed toward the exit.

Ananda watched her walk away then let her eyes move around the room taking in her surroundings. Her eyes halted when they connected with friendly pair of chestnut brown eyes that were staring directly at her; seemingly looking deeply enough to touch her very soul. Breaking the magnetic connection of their eyes meeting when the waiter returned she graciously smiled when she and Tracey's food was placed on the table.

After Tracey hadn't returned after five minutes Ananda picked up her fork and dug into her food focusing instead on an inhibited woman now on the stage telling about living life on the streets in the midst of prostitution and drugs.

"It's a great story she's telling." A deep voice with a slight southern accent spoke from behind her.

Startled Ananda spun around in her seat to see who was interrupting her leisure time. The man staring down at her smiled and she soon realized that it was the man with the friendly eyes.

"Trust me, it's a good story. I know her personally." Ananda gazed into his chestnut brown eyes and wondered what made him think that she cared whether he knew the woman personally or not. All she was interested in was a good story that could entertain her for a little while.

Glancing around the restaurant bustling with noisy patrons seeking a break from work, school or just life in general, eager to hear the next artist, Ananda wondered why this mystery guy had approached her. Ananda guessed him to be around six feet tall, not bad on the eyes and he reminded her of a younger, curly-headed version of Idris Elba.

"Is that so?" Ananda said coyly, "And what makes you think that I'd be impressed just because you know the woman on stage?" She studied him intently, "I don't even know you, so why should that move me any?"

"That's my fault." He smiled down at her and stuck out his right, "I'm Malcolm and you'll get to know me."

Ananda rolled her eyes at his cockiness and thought about ignoring his hand, but her mother hadn't raised her to be rude so she took his hand into hers. "Ananda." she said immediately withdrawing her hand away from his after she introduced herself.

Malcolm couldn't help laughing at her snappiness. Ananda eyed him warily.

"Are you laughing at me?"

"Not at all. I'm just enjoying the view." Malcolm said with sincerity in his voice. He hadn't lied to her; he was definitely enjoying his view. He could tell that she was tired, but even tired she looked good to him. He couldn't help admiring her curves in the form fitting blue sundress that she had on which radiated perfectly off her brown skin, with her sunglasses pushed on top of her curly head. He loved a curvy woman. She was short, but he liked that and there was something about her haunted sad brown eyes that drew him in and made him want to know everything about her.

"Thank you for letting me know that you know the presenter for whatever reason." She told him with a hint of sarcasm.

"I'm actually an agent." He handed her his business card. "And I think that you have an amazing look, so maybe you'll think about letting me represent you and in the meantime use my number for whatever else suits you." He told her suggestively.

Ananda gave a tired laugh as she shook her head, Malcolm was persistent she had to give him that. "An agent huh?" She asked looking at his business card.

"Yes." He focused intense brown eyes on her, "I represent models and I'm telling you, you have what it takes. I know you're taking me as a joke right now, but I never play about money."

Ananda knew he was serious, she also knew that he was dying for her to give him an opportunity to take her out.

"Okay, okay." She giggled, "You've persuaded me. Take my number as well in case I get tied up and neglect to call." Malcolm was only too eager to pull out his cell phone. After reciting ten digits off to him, he politely excused himself and she continued eating her dinner waiting for Tracey to come back from taking her phone call.

Later that evening Ananda lay in bed dressed in cotton Betty Boop pajama pants, a white tank top and a leopard print scarf wrapped around her head. She finally had a moment to herself to relax and couldn't have been happier. Leaning her head back into her plush Ralph Lauren pillow, she turned the TV on to *Chelsea Lately* with the volume on low as she laughed at the sarcastic free for all of Chelsea and her fellow guest comedians as they ravaged other celebrities and topics of the day.

Her cell pinging with an indication of a newly delivered text message forced Ananda to break away from gazing at the television. Sitting up to retrieve her phone from the nightstand she was amazed to see that three hours had gone by since she had first begun watching. The time was steadily approaching midnight and considering she had to leave for work at six in the morning she knew she was going to regret losing these precious hours of slumber. Seeing that the text wasn't from someone whose number was stored in her phone Ananda became skeptical about who would be texting her so late.

"Thinking about me?" Ananda couldn't help but smile when she read the message knowing that it could be no one other than Malcolm.

"Um, do you know what time it is? It is rude to text someone you just met a few hours ago this late?" Ananda laughed as she pushed send on her Android. If nothing else, she was going to teach Mister Malcolm the correct etiquette when trying to deal with her.

Ananda couldn't believe Malcolm's audacity once the phone began to ring in her hand.

"I see someone has neglected to teach you manners." Ananda's sarcasm oozed from every word when she answered the call.

"Thought you were a big girl, or do you have a curfew?" Malcolm shot back at her.

"Oh, so now you're trying to be smart?" Ananda laughed into the phone.

"No, not at all, I'm just trying to find out if you were thinking about me."

"Definitely was not thinking about you." Ananda said, "Does that answer your question?"

"Yes, but I've accomplished what I intended because you're thinking about me now." Malcolm said smoothly ignoring her smart remarks.

Ananda burst into laughter she couldn't help herself. She could see that Malcolm was determined to make her a part of his world and who was she to stand in his way.

"Ok, I'm thinking about you. Are you happy now?"

"Yes. That's all I was wanted."

"But you are aware that it is now after midnight. I don't have a curfew, but I am a working woman and I must get ready to head to sleep."

"My apologies, I don't want to stop your beauty rest. Are you free two weekends from now? I'll be back in town, so I'll come out there to visit you."

"Wait, you don't live here?" Malcolm had Ananda's undivided attention at this point.

"No. I'm from Atlanta, but I do a lot of business in Maryland, so I'm here quite often."

My Boyfriend's Wife

"Oh okay. I may be free that weekend, but I'll have to let you know about me taking you in as a houseguest and everything. You may try and take advantage of me or something."

"I'm absolutely going to take advantage of you." Malcolm laughed on his end of the phone, "But trust me, you are going to thoroughly enjoy it."

"I'll keep you posted on that. Have a good night."

"Before you kick me off the phone make sure you dream about me aight."

"Boy, get outta here." Ananda laughed, "Good night." She said hanging up the phone. She could tell now that Malcolm was going to be a piece of work.

****

"Why am I just now hearing about this mystery guy you met two weeks after the fact?"

"Because I wasn't ready to talk about him yet and I wasn't sure if I was going to really entertain his advances or not."

"So what's changed?" Ananda loved how blunt her friend Tracey could be.

"I don't know. He's different from the guys here. He's so honest and I really like that about him."

"Mmmm 'kay. You just be careful. I worry about you."

"What you worried about me for?" Ananda eyed her strangely.

"Because you love so hard and not one guy you have loved has ever been good for you. Not one."

Ananda hated to admit it, but she knew that Tracey was right.

"I know Tray, but I gotta have hope, you know? What am I supposed to do, stay single forever?"

"No, I just don't want my friend being taken advantage of you know. You're like a sister to me and every time you go through these breakups you're never the same after. Every single one of these guys is slowly changing you."

Ananda stared out of the bay window in her den thinking back about Braxton. And then her mind wandered back to her last serious relationship before him that ended in her abruptly moving to a new apartment with no money and pretty much starving for two months. Her ex-boyfriend had been abusive in every sense of the word physically, mentally, spiritually and any way you could think of. She'd hated going home at night after work, she'd hated her job, everything had become too much for her and soon she began spiraling into a depression. Ananda was all too familiar with the symptoms. She had suffered a bout of depression in her early college days after dealing with yet another boyfriend who had been physically abusive and cheated on her with every woman with a vagina.

Ananda knew there was truth to what Tracey was saying, but she was an optimist and she believed that her one was out there. She couldn't isolate herself from men forever. In order to win you have to play the game. That was the motto that she stood by and is what she continues to believe in even after all of the hurt and disappointment she has endured.

"I know Tray, but with each one I learn a little more about me."

"I hear you, just be sure to take care of you, okay?" Tracey said, not trying to be the pessimist but genuinely wanting Ananda to be happy. But still she worried, because she always seemed to attract the worst guys.

"Yes Mom I got this." Ananda said laughing. Tracey was forever thinking she was someone's mother and always knew best.

"Okay, smarty pants since you not listening to my speech anyway, tell me all about him."

"He's so great. Why don't you just come over and meet him when he comes to town this weekend. He'll be staying at my place."

"Overnight company so soon? You sure that's a good idea?"

"Aight Tracey, enough. I heard you the first time. I'm going to do what I want to do okay. Just chill a little bit dag."

"Don't go getting frustrated with me. I'm trying to be the voice of reason over here."

"Can you be that a little more quietly please?" Ananda asked her.

"Fine, you won't hear another word from me about what a bad decision this is."

"Tray worry about your man okay. Where is Cameron anyway?"

"Hey leave Cam out of this." Tracey was immediately on the defensive because her ongoing drama with Cameron and dealing with their own issues.

"See, doesn't feel so great right? Leave me to mine and I'll leave you to yours."

"Point taken. I'll come over and meet the great guy this weekend. What's his name again?"

"Malcolm, his name is Malcolm."

Tracey dialed Cameron's number for the fifth time in a half hour before finally throwing the phone at the wall in the family room when she received his voicemail message again. Watching her cell hit the taupe wall with a loud bang and shatter onto the hardwood floor made Tracey angry. This is not what she signed up for when she'd married Cameron. She knew that he was a hot commodity for groupies since he played basketball for the Wizards, but she was his wife and demanded respect no matter the circumstances that brought them together. Grabbing the keys to her black 2010 Lexus and black purse off of her Muschio oval coffee table, Tracey headed out the front door of her and Cameron's two-story house in the Bowie, Maryland neighborhood of Woodmore.

Climbing in, she started her car and Tracey was immediately serenaded with Hezekiah Walker's hit song, *God Favored Me*. Cutting the power on her radio Tracey felt anything but favored at the moment, she felt like she was spiraling out of control. Trying to force herself to drive slowly on Route 50, she attempted to calm herself down, but recognized that she was hoping and wishing on a broken star. Feeling her heart quicken as she passed the Welcome to Washington, DC sign, Tracey navigated to one of the more economically challenged sections of Southeast DC and began praying with all her might. Passing by a homeless man sitting on a gray five-quart paint bucket waving his hat from side to side hoping that someone would put change into it, she knew her prayer had been in vain. The man sitting on the paint bucket was posted up across from a Black QX56 Infinity truck with the license plate "CAM 2 U" in front of Meadow Run Apartments on 6th

Street. Grateful that there was an open parking space right behind his truck Tracey parked her Lexus and jumped out the car. In a full on sprint, Tracey made it to the top of the hill to the apartment building in no time. Hopping the steps two at a time Tracey banged on the door like a crazy person when she made it to apartment 319.

"What in the world!" Tracey heard a female voice yell out.

"You know who it is! Cam you get out here right now! Or I swear I will break this door down!" Tracey yelled at the top of her lungs.

"Excuse me Miss, but you can't come over here making all that noise." Tracey spun around angrily to face the speaker. It was an older lady with her hair in rollers on the opposite side of the hall that had opened her door a crack to see what the commotion was. "A nice young lady lives there with her son."

"I'm sorry to disturb you ma'am." Tracey began as she tried to remain respectful and in control of her raging emotions at the same time. "But nice young ladies don't mess around with married men, so I am sorry to disturb you, but please mind your business. Thank you." Tracey said before spinning around to bang on the door again.

"Cameron if you don't open this door right this second I am coming in there to get you!" She yelled kicking the heavy burgundy door with all her might causing the door knocker to shake.

The door squeaked open slowly and all six foot three of Cameron strolled out in blue jeans with a tank top on showcasing his well-defined muscles and his white t-shirt hung around his neck with a Redskins fitted cap on his head acting like he didn't have a care in the world with a angry scowl on his face.

"Why you over here acting like a crazy person?" Cameron demanded of Tracey in a low irritated tone.

"Why are you over here at all!" Tracey shouted at the top of her lungs, "You have some nerve."

Cameron grabbed Tracey's arms in a vice grip and yanked her up off her feet so all five foot four of her could look him in his eyes, "If you ever do this again I promise you won't like the consequences." He said in a menacing tone as he abruptly let her go and she fell to the dirty concrete floor outside of the apartment door. Stepping over her Cameron made his way down the stairs toward his truck.

Humiliated, Tracey glanced up to see the woman that Cameron had been shacked up with standing in her doorway looking down on her. Jumping up Tracey stuck her foot in the doorway as the woman tried to shove it closed in her face.

Pushing the door hard the woman leapt backwards from the power of the push and the door banged against the wall. Tracey stepped close to the woman sticking her finger in the woman's face, "You stay away from my husband you hear me! If I find him here again I will kill you, do you understand me?" Tracey screeched. She was angry to the point of shaking.

The woman shook her head at Tracey with a solemn look on her face. She didn't want any problems, "If he decides to come I will let him in." She said meekly with her head bowed down. Tracey jumped in the woman's face, "You must be stupid, but that's okay," She kicked the door closed as she fully entered the apartment, "All that is about to change." She said and slowly approached the woman with fists raised.

Later that evening Tracey finally made it home and was still livid. Entering the house she shared with Cameron all she wanted to do was bash his head in when she found him in the basement movie room watching old reruns of Martin on the projection screen laughing like everything was cool. Turning Tracey walked down the hall to the electrical box and flipped the power switch for the movie room.

"What did you do? The power just went out in here." Cameron yelled. Making her way back down the hall to the darkened room Tracey stood in the doorway illuminated by the hall light and stared at Cameron.

"So you think you're just going to get away with what happened tonight?" Tracey eyed Cameron as if he were stupid. "You had some nerve trying to pull that mess you did today in DC."

"Look," Cameron said standing up to walk toward her, "I'm not in the mood for this today. You had no business showing up where you didn't belong." He tried to move past her.

Tracey blocked the exit and refused to budge out of his way. "You are married! I belong wherever my husband is and your place isn't over there, it is here with me. I better not find you over there again. Do you hear me?"

Cameron snatched Tracey up by the waist and brought her in close to him, "You listen to me and please listen to me very carefully." He spoke while their brown eyes collided, "I will do as I please and if you want to remain in the lifestyle that you have been afforded you will do well to know your place." Cameron abruptly let her go, "Don't forget where I saved you from. You are my wife and I love you, but I will do as I damn well please and don't you forget that. I meant what I said, show up over there again and you won't like the consequences."

Tracey narrowed her eyes and bit her tongue forcing back tears unwilling to give Cameron the satisfaction of seeing her cry.

"You've gone and ruined my night, think I'll head back to the city. I may see you tomorrow if not, please don't interrupt me. You know where I am, call if you need me." Cameron stated as he bounded up the basement stairs.

Tracey waited until she heard Cameron's truck start up outside before she made a move. Cameron thought she should be complacent just because he felt as if he rescued her, but Tracey had another thing coming for him. She was not going to be a victim and he wasn't going to continually throw her past life back in her face. It just wasn't going to happen.

Five

*M*alcolm sat on the edge of the bed feeling like a piece of crap. Glancing over his shoulder observing Heather sleeping peacefully on the King-sized bed next to him with her long hair fanned out over the pillows around her face, he felt even worse. Standing slowly he gathered his clothes off the floor, took them into the large bathroom forcing himself to dress as quickly as possible. Opening the door as quietly as he could without disturbing Heather, Malcolm searched for his keys in the dark room.

"Looking for these?" He jumped at the sound of a husky voiced Heather, dangling the keys from her finger in the dark room. Her silhouette illuminated only by the moonlight shimmering through the silk curtains that hung from the large windows as she sat up in the bed to glare at his failed attempt to slip out quietly into the night.

Malcolm glanced up in feigned shock at the bed. "I thought you were asleep."

"I was till I heard you get up." Heather replied eyeing Malcolm intently, "Where are you headed at this ungodly hour?" Her eyes zoomed in on the digital clock in her room that read 4:17.

Malcolm stared at Heather angry with himself for spending the night in the first place. "Can I have my keys?" He asked, ignoring her question, "It's none of your business where I'm headed. Let me have my keys." He was beginning to get frustrated because he didn't have time for these games.

"You can have them once you let me know where you are going."

"I don't have time for this." Malcolm quickly walked out of Heather's master bedroom headed for the stairs. She could keep those keys as far as he was concerned. He kept a spare set of keys in a little compartment he'd had installed under his car, just in case he ever lost them. He was willing to take a loss today.

Heather ran after Malcolm with the sheet wrapped around her nude body and tried to cut him off at the stairs but he had already made it to the front door.

"Wait! What about your keys?"

Malcolm looked back up at her as she stood at the top of the stairs holding his keys hostage, with the sheet wrapped around her petite body. If he hadn't been trying to leave he would have thought she looked sexy as her wavy hair cascaded down her back. "You can keep them as a souvenir for yourself. I have to go."

"What does that mean? You're not coming back?" Heather whined.

Malcolm stepped out the front door and closed it behind him. He heard a loud clank on the other side of the door and figured Heather must have thrown the keys. He was indifferent at this point as he jogged to his black on black Audi S7. Retrieving his spare keys from the box under his car next to his left back tire, he had slid into his car when Heather, still wrapped in her sheet, indignantly marched out the front door with fire in her eyes.

Malcolm stepped back out the car and began walking toward her, "Woman get your naked ass back in the house right now! Out here with no clothes on -- are you crazy?" Now she had him upset to the point he wanted to choke her.

"Not until you come back inside." Heather snapped back at him, "You are not going to just leave me like this."

Roughing snatching her arm into a vise grip, Malcolm didn't care if he hurt her or not. "Are you crazy?" He growled at her as he half dragged her and she half tripped back toward the house abruptly letting her go when he noticed that neighbors had begun cutting on their porch lights and looking out their windows. "So you trying to get me arrested or something? Huh?" When they reached the front door he shoved her inside and used his spare key to lock her in.

Malcolm was livid as he made his way back to his car. Heather acting out had completely ruined his morning.

****

"I'm happy you came back." Merci smiled when she saw Malcolm come through the door. She had been lying on the cream leather sofa under a throw blanket in the living room waiting for him to come home.

Malcolm returned her smile as he took his shoes off leaving them at the door and started moving down the hall to check in on a sleeping Caprice. Entering his daughter's pink and purple painted room that was completely engulfed in LaLa Loopsy paraphernalia, Malcolm's mood shifted to a better place as he glanced down at Caprice in her bed. She had thrown the covers off and the top part of her body was on the mattress while her legs were hanging off almost touching the floor. Gently picking up her legs and putting them back on the bed, Malcolm grabbed her LaLa Loopsy comforter and pulled it up under her chin. He didn't understand how children could sleep so erratic like that. Leaning down to place a soft kiss on her cheek, he silently pulled the door to and headed back down the hall to engage with Merci.

Malcolm sat on the floor in front of Merci and placed his head on the sofa. Merci reached up and began to rub his head.

"You tired?' She asked. Malcolm nodded, "Well that's what you get running the street all hours of the night."

Malcolm took in a deep breath, "That's not why I'm tired." He said as he rose to his feet and stared down at her.

"Okay, so what's the problem?"

He knew Merci loved him. He had known her for ten years and during those ten years they'd had their share of ups and downs, but he'd spent the last three years in turmoil trying to figure out how to break things off with her. He couldn't deny that she was a good woman, but she wasn't the woman for him.

"I need some space."

Merci cut her eyes at Malcolm. "Space to do what?" Her tone just moments before that had been lighthearted was now low and calculating.

Malcolm knew that a fight was coming. It was inevitable with Merci. She was from the streets and she didn't play a lot of games, especially when it came to her man.

Malcolm cleared his throat. He didn't want any problems with Merci, Caprice was his main concern and he didn't want to do or say anything that would have Merci make it hard to continue seeing her.

"Space between me and you. I'm out doing me anyway and it's not fair to you." Malcolm figured honesty was the best way to approach this situation. Honesty was something that Merci could appreciate.

"But I figured at some point you would reel that in. And you're telling me now, after I've spent all these years waiting for you that you have no intention of strengthening our relationship." Merci's voice began to escalate as she rose up off the sofa so she could stand face to face with Malcolm.

Malcolm knew a threat when he saw one. Merci was about to take a fighting stance so she could begin to throw blows. Reaching for her arms he held them by her side so he wouldn't have to go into defense mode and swing back on her. He could see the hurt in her eyes and didn't want to hurt her more.

"I'm really sorry, but I can't keep playing this game with you. I met someone and I want to be able to date her without feeling guilty about having you at home waiting for me.

Merci's eyes flashed as she fought to pull her arms free so that she could bash Malcolm's skull in.

"This has to do with that woman that you met in D.C. doesn't it?" Merci questioned him, "Her name is Ananda right?"

Malcolm's face reflected his confusion because he wasn't sure how Merci knew anything about Ananda.

"You're not good at keeping secrets." She told him seeing the look on his face. "I've been with you for ten years and you do this to me?" Merci's eyes began to tear heavily.

Seeing the tears Malcolm let Merci's arms go and lifted his hands to her face.

As soon as Merci felt Malcolm let her arms go she punched him in the eye.

"Are you crazy? Did you think I was going to take that sitting down." She yelled at him as he held his eye with one hand and balled up his fist with the other.

"Yeah, I dare you to say something with your selfish ass. I dare you." Merci was bouncing around Malcolm in their living room taunting him as if she were Muhammad Ali in the ring.

Malcolm took his hand away from his eye and began a slow walk toward Merci and his patience was officially gone so he didn't care about her or her feelings at this point.

Merci stood her ground. He has some nerve she thought. Malcolm reached both hands out picking Merci up in one scoop and throwing her onto the sofa. Getting on top of her Malcolm brought his hands to her throat as Merci struggled beneath him.

"Daddy." A small sleepy voice called out.

Malcolm halted at the sound of the tiny voice and glanced up to see Caprice standing in the doorway watching him and her mom. Willing his body to relax Malcolm stood up off Merci.

"What are you doing to Mommy?"

"Nothing princess." He told her as he walked over to her and gathered her up in his arms. "We were playing a game that's all."

Caprice hugged Malcolm around his neck, "Can I play too?" She asked innocently.

"Not this game boo. What are you doing up so early?" He asked hoping to change the subject.

"You and Mommy were loud and woke me up." She told him simply. "I'm hungry Daddy." Malcolm laughed at the attention span of children

"You are? Well what do you want for breakfast?" He asked as he carried her to the kitchen.

Merci waited until they had retreated to the kitchen before sitting up on the sofa. She was ready to kill Malcolm. If he thought she was going to take this lying down then he had another thing coming. She didn't care that he had took it upon himself to call off their engagement years prior. They had continued to live together and be in a relationship so they were still engaged as far as she was concerned and come hell or high water they would be getting married and soon.

$\mathcal{S}ix$

"$\mathcal{L}$orna." Hunter called out to her in a callous tone, "how is that networking event coming along?" Ever since returning from Miami, Hunter had intentionally put distance between him and Lorna. He was usually cautious about mixing business with pleasure, so he was more disappointed with himself than anything. He felt like he had let himself down not being able to live up to his own standards.

Lorna looked up at Hunter standing in the doorway of his office staring at her. She was surprised that he was speaking to her in person and not through email. Ever since their encounter he'd barely spoken two words to her.

"It's going well." She responded, "I've finally locked down a venue and received RSVP's from your massive guest list.

"That's great" He told her as he saw her begin to blush under his gaze. "Can you come into my office so we can address a few things?" He turned and reentered his office not waiting for a response.

Lorna jumped up when he said for her to come into his office. Even though he'd worded it like a question she knew that it was more of a command and she knew that he didn't like to be kept waiting.

"Yes sir." Lorna responded as she entered the office. "What can I do for you?"

"Please shut the door and have a seat." He told her motioning at the two chairs arranged in front of his desk in his regal office. Hunter had the office made up to satisfy his love of the arts and culture. It had taken a few months, but he now had it arranged exactly how he wanted. His company was located in an impressive glass building in New York City on the Avenue of the Americas and occupied the entire fifth floor. They'd just emerged from a lucrative fiscal year and Hunter figured it was a great time for expansion and a few upgrades, so he'd had an interior decorator come in and maximize the space on the floor. He loved coming into his office, but right now he had more pressing matters to attend to than relishing his office space. First point of business on his to-do list was Lorna.

Lorna did as told and wondered what he wanted to speak with her about. Getting comfortable in the chair she waited for him to speak.

"I want to talk to you about Miami." Hunter began, "I don't want there to be any confusion between us. It never should have happened. I apologize for the part I played in it and I would like us to remain on professional terms in and out of the office."

"Yes sir." Lorna quickly agreed, "I never expected anything to come out of it. It was just one night."

"Yes one night of supreme bad judgment on both our parts." Hunter clapped his hands together good, "I'm glad that we are in agreement. That's all I needed from you, just wanted to make sure that we were on the same page."

"Yes sir, same page." Lorna said as she stood trying to hurry out the office so that Hunter wouldn't see the tears that were threatening to fall from her face. She had been foolish to hope that their one night could hopefully turn into more, but she would make sure that one day he saw her as worthy of his love and attention. If nothing else, Hunter was going to want another taste of his strawberry Lorna.

Seven

"You came right in time for the fireworks." Ananda exclaimed. She was excited and loving Malcolm's company. His flight had come in around seven and now they were standing on the walkway over the water on the Wilson Bridge looking waiting for the close of the city's July 4th celebration. It was dark and Ananda was anticipating the show of fireworks that would shortly light up the clear summer sky.

Malcolm gazed down at Ananda and smiled. Being with her was easy as she made him feel comfortable and at peace.

"Oh yeah?" He commented, "I've never been to see the fireworks show on the Mall before, so this is new for me."

"Are you serious?" Ananda was genuinely stunned as she stared up at him. She figured everyone had gone at least once in their lifetime or at least seen them televised.

"Yeah, but I'm enjoying this."

"As you should" Ananda teased. While the two of them stood on the bridge Ananda was grateful that they were over the water because it helped when a breeze came through to cut the heat and humidity. Even though she was rocking a short denim skirt, pink tank top and flip flops she felt as if she was about to melt alive. Doing her best to keep her sexy going while she began to perspire, she looked over to see how Malcolm was faring in the stifling July heat. Taking him in from head to toe he looked good to her and she didn't see a drop of sweat on him. He was wearing black cargo shorts, a white t-shirt and black and white Adidas Crazy 8's on his feet.

"I don't understand it." She whispered.

"What?" He asked.

"How are you managing to keep from sweating in this heat? I feel like my body is on fire from the inside out. I'm roasting alive over here."

Malcolm laughed at Ananda's indignation; he thought she looked cute and very summery in her outfit. The little drops of sweat he saw on her nose were endearing. He reached over and gently wiped away the few drops of sweat.

"I'm from Atlanta, remember? It gets much hotter there. I'm used to it."

"Please, the dog days of summer in D.C. are legendary and even though I've lived here my whole life I'm still not used to it."

Malcolm smiled, "Shhh and look." He said as he pointed to the first pink spray that illuminated the evening sky. Ananda's eyes lit up, so caught up in the heat and Malcolm she hadn't heard the first firework pop off she was elated the fireworks had begun – and not just those overhead.

When she and Malcolm made it back to her apartment, Ananda was exhausted. She had originally thought that she would cook dinner for him, but that was out of the question now. She just wanted to lie down, but her ringing cell phone stopped her.

"Hey Tray, what's good?"

"Cameron is an asshole, but we already knew that. Is your guy in town yet?"

"Yes Malcolm is here." Ananda answered intentionally ignoring the Cameron remark. She was too tired to get into that with Tracey tonight.

"Good. I'm going to come over."

Ananda checked the time on her cell it was going on a quarter to eleven. "Tray, we're tired. Can you come in the morning?"

"Girl please, it's still early and you don't have to work tomorrow. I'm on my way."

Ananda sighed as she glanced down at the screen when Tracey hung up. This wasn't about Malcolm, Tracey wanted to get over here to talk about whatever was bugging her about Cameron.

"Everything okay?" Malcolm asked still standing in the living room with his bags.

"Yes, that was just my girl Tracey, she's on her way over to meet you. I hope you don't mind."

"Nah, it's cool."

"Good because I really don't feel like fighting with her about it tonight. Come let me show you where you can put your things." Ananda remarked as she guided him to her guest room.

Tracey knocked on Ananda's door exactly twenty minutes later. She normally would have used her key, but because

Malcolm was there she wanted to be respectful of Ananda's company.

Ananda opened the door slowly. "Can we make introductions fast? I really just want to go to sleep."

"Ana don't be that way. Let me meet your new guy and then I have to tell you what's up with Cameron."

Ananda groaned inwardly. She wasn't in the mood for this tonight she knew Tracey coming over was a set up and the only entertaining Ananda wanted to partake in was Malcolm.

"Malcolm this is Tracey. Tracey Malcolm." Ananda introduced them as she yawned.

Tracey tried to hide her reaction when Malcolm rose off of the sofa to greet her. She had to give it to Ananda, the brother was handsome.

"So you're the mysterious Malcolm I've just recently heard about." She said as she shook his hand. "I see why Ananda was keeping you a secret."

"Tracey hush, and let Malcolm's hand go," said Ananda rolling her eyes, she was trying to think of a reason to get Tracey out of her place. "Malcolm I'm sorry, can you give us a few minutes?" Ananda asked him as she excused herself and Tracey to go into her bedroom.

"Tray what is going on?" Ananda wasted no time beating around the bush as she lay on her bed. The sooner they got to the root of the problem the sooner Tracey would be on her way back home.

"Cameron is acting a fool." Tracey said as she began pacing the length of Ananda's room.

"So why are you here and not at home trying to work it out?"

"Because he's not there." Tracey replied, her voice barely above a whisper.

Ananda glanced at the digital clock on her nightstand that read 11:36 pm. "Well where is he?"

"At his mistress' place."

Sitting up abruptly Ananda wasn't sure if she heard right, "I'm sorry, where?"

"You heard me." Tracey said, "He's at his mistress' place."

"Tray, what in the world? You have never mentioned anything about a mistress. You're okay with this?" Ananda eyed her indignantly.

Tracey looked at Ananda as if she were crazy, "You know I'm not okay with it, but he made it clear that it's either accept it or he's probably going to put me out."

"Wait." Ananda laughed in disbelief not knowing what else to do. "This is craziness Tray. I mean really. How long has this been going on?"

Tracey shrugged her shoulders as she studied the designs in Ananda's comforter ashamed that she was allowing this foolery to take place. "About a year or so."

"WHAT!" Ananda was shocked. She knew Tracey and Cameron had their issues, but she had no idea that he had taken a mistress and had been seeing her for the last year. "A whole year and this is your first time mentioning it to me. Tray, are you crazy? You know you don't have to put up with this."

"What would you suggest I do? I'm not going back to living the way that I used to live. I can't. Cameron really did save me. I owe him."

Ananda looked at Tracey as if she had lost her mind. This wasn't her loud and boisterous friend-- this woman was emotionally battered the same way she was. She usually forgot about Tracey's past because she was so busy putting up such a tough front.

"Tracey, you don't owe Cameron anything. He did not save you, you saved yourself. Cam allowed you the means to do it, but you're the one that ultimately made the choice to change your life. Don't you dare let him use that against you and make it seem like you don't have the right to be upset about him taking a mistress. You have every right to be angry and upset. This isn't even happening to me and I'm angry. He cannot do this to you, do you hear me? I need the Tracey that's always trying to be my momma to step up to the plate and handle this situation. If you need to leave Cam you know that you can always come and stay with me. I will always have space for my sister, you understand me?" Ananda asked Tracey as she pulled her friend into a hug. For the life of her she couldn't understand men. They could have the perfect woman and that wasn't good enough for them. Not all men, but some.

"Everything you say is right, but I don't know what to do." Tracey pulled out of Ananda's embrace. "He hadn't been home in two days, he hadn't been answering his phone or anything, so today I had had enough. I got into my car and drove to his mistress' apartment."

"You know where she lives?"

"I've known where she's lives for a while now. One night I followed him over there to see where he was going all the time."

Ananda was at a loss for words, she'd had no idea that her friend had been going through all of this. While Tracey had been lecturing her about her man issues, she should have heeded some of her own advice.

"Anyway, as soon as I pull into her neighborhood I see his truck parked on the street. I parked right behind him and went and knocked on her door and sure enough his insensitive ass comes waltzing out her apartment like it's any other day and everything is cool. Like his wife isn't out standing in front of his mistress' door. I did not sign up for this with Cameron. We made a deal when we got married; he was supposed to protect me from this type of thing."

Ananda was all too familiar with the ways of men. Every boyfriend she'd had had cheated on her. Every single one, but she knew in her heart that all men weren't the same. She and Tracey were just having a run of bad luck, that's all.

"Tracey you need to talk to him and see what the problem is. Do you still want to be married?"

"Of course I want to be married. I love Cam, but I know I'm not going to be able to deal with him cheating on me for the rest of my life. It's just not going to happen. And what's crazy, it's not even like a onetime thing, he has developed a relationship with this woman. This is someone that he has feelings for. You don't spend a year with somebody and not have feelings, it just doesn't happen."

"I don't know." Ananda said. Guys are funny like that. He just may enjoy having sex with her."

"Gee that makes it so much better. Thanks." Tracey remarked sarcastically.

Ananda tilted her head to the side as she gazed into Tracey's sad eyes. "Okay, so what's the plan because I know your brain is working overtime."

Tracey gave a devious smile, "Well, I've been thinking."

Ananda shook her head. "I knew this was coming."

"How about we do a drive by?"

"What type of drive by and for what?" Ananda was exasperated. She knew Tracey was about that street life and it's not that she wasn't down because normally she would be all in, but she had company in the other room that she really wanted to spend time with.

"A get your butt home before I kill you drive by."

"Tonight?" Ananda began shaking her head even more, "Tray I can't. I have company remember? How am I supposed to explain to him that I'm running out to do a drive by on your husband's mistress without looking crazy?"

"So you're not coming?" Tracey's face showed how crushed she felt that her friend would abandon her at a time like this when she needed her the most, "You know that I would do it for you."

"I know that you would and normally I would be down for the cause, but I have company." Ananda said beginning to feel like a broken record because she had to keep repeating herself. "It would be rude of me to roll out with you and leave Malcolm here alone. I'm not doing it. But Monday if this is still going down, you know I am there."

"Monday isn't good enough! We are going tonight Ana." Tracey screamed hysterically. "If the situation was reversed, no matter what I was doing I would be there with you and you know it."

Ananda leaned her head back and gazed up at her ceiling noticing a crack beginning, she made a mental note to call the leasing office first thing Monday morning to get it fixed. She sighed.

"Aight, let's go."

Tracey's face lit up like the Christmas Tree at Rockefeller Center. "I knew you were my girl. Thank you."

Ananda was beyond words at the moment. She slowly got up off her bed and opened her bedroom door trying to figure out what she was going to tell Malcolm.

****

Looking out the window as they drove into the city Ananda was exhausted and wishing that she'd taken a shot of vodka before beginning this excursion with Tracey. Glancing at her while she drove life a maniac through the narrow streets having the car jerking every two seconds it seemed to Ananda because she kept running up on cars in front of her going a lightning speed, then having to slam on breaks.

"Can you slow down a little? It would be awesome if I didn't have to go to the hospital for whiplash tonight." Ananda said to her sarcastically.

"Oh." Tracey gradually let her foot up from the accelerator. "I'm sorry Ana, I'm just anxious to get there and catch up with Cameron."

"I understand that, but are you sure you sure you really want to do this? We can still turn back you know."

"We're not turning back." Tracey exclaimed furiously. "I'm sick of Cameron thinking he can do any and everything that he wants to do with no repercussions. All of that's about to change tonight. I've had it with all this stepping out. Not happening."

"Okay." A defeated Ananda replied. She was all too aware of how Tracey could get, so she had nothing else to say about the matter. She was glad that Malcolm could be so understanding about her having to make a street run with her crazy friend who was so on edge that she was about to pop a vessel. But he'd said that he understood and she was happy about that, even though she felt as if it were a bad first impression for his weekend visit with her.

The car screeched to a halt in front of some apartments. Ananda figured they must have arrived.

"Let's go." Tracey stated as she opened the car door and hopped out her Lexus. Ananda followed her lead watching as Tracey strolled to the back of the car and popped the trunk pulling out a knife.

"What's that for?" Tracey had Ananda apprehensive now, fighting someone was one thing, but she wasn't signing up to be an accessory if Tracey lost it and murdered Cam and the girl. "Tray don't be thinking of nothing crazy."

"Will you calm down? I'm not going to stab them." She paused, "At least that's not the plan, I don't think." She winked at Ananda.

"Don't be winking at me, I'm not playing with you. I am not going to be a witness." Ananda told her in all seriousness.

"Really Ethel, you have got to relax." Tracey smiled at her.

"Okay Lucy you just don't get us in trouble this time please."
Ananda smiled back at Tracey shaking her head. Reminiscing
back on the days when they had been children and how much they
had enjoyed watching *I Love Lucy*.

"You see Cameron's truck right there?" Tracey asked as they
began walking up the street and she pointed directly in front of
them.

Ananda saw the truck with the tags CAM 2 U and groaned.

"This," Tracey said holding up the knife is for his tires she
announced as she jogged to the truck and stabbed the knife in
several places till all four tires were flat.

"Chick you have some loose marbles up there you know?"
Ananda said pointing at her head.

Tracey smiled, "This way he can't make a quick getaway like
last time."

Ananda didn't say anything she just wanted to get this over
with so that she could get back to Malcolm. Even though he was
nice, he was still a stranger in a sense and she had left him alone in
her apartment. She wondered if he was a snooper. She hoped not
because she didn't need him going through her stuff.

Ananda followed Tracey up the stairs to the unit the woman
lived in and stood off to the side of the woman's door so that she
couldn't be seen through the peephole.

Tracey knocked on the door and quickly stepped to the other
side of the door staring straight at Ananda. They could hear
muffled voices coming from inside the apartment and footsteps as
someone came to the door.

"Who is it?" They heard Cameron's voice ring out. Ananda's
eyes widened as she stared at Tracey who remained silent and

pointed at her. Ananda shook her head as she could feel the anger radiating of Tracey, she knew she wanted to knock the door off the hinges. Ananda knew Tracey wanted her to say that it was her knocking so that Cameron would open the door.

Ananda sighed and stepped in front of the peephole seeing that Tracey wasn't going to budge and trying not to prolong the evening.

"It's Ananda Cam. Something is up with Tracey and she told me that I may be able to find you here."

Cameron opened the door once she said something was up with Tracey. "What's wrong with Tracey?" He asked genuinely concerned, but before Ananda could say a word Tracey came from the side of the door and charged him with enough force that they both landed on the floor inside the apartment.

Ananda heard a scream as she looked up and saw a nude woman running up to Cameron quickly stepping in front of the woman Ananda pushed her away.

"You need to back up." Ananda told her as Tracey and Cameron were struggling on the floor.

"No, you need to get out of my apartment."

"I don't need to do anything, but we will gladly leave once these two sort out their differences." Ananda looked directly into the woman's eyes, "I don't want to have to hurt you, so please stand back and let them work through this." Ananda politely insisted.

"No forget that. It's not going down in my place." The woman told her as she bucked at Ananda with a raised fist.

Without further conversation, Ananda jabbed the woman in her throat and watched as she crumbled to the floor gasping for air and then blacking out. Ananda shook her head, she hated people to talk a lot of nonsense and not be able to back it up. Stepping over the stupid woman, she focused her attention on Tracey and Cameron. Cameron had Tracey pinned to the floor as he smacked her.

"Hey get off of her!" Ananda screamed as she jumped on Cameron's back and began punching him. "Are you crazy? This is your wife!"

Cameron easily threw Ananda off of him where she landed on the hardwood floor with a loud thud as her head bounced off the floor.

"I am your wife!" Tracey yelled, "You will not disrespect me like this. You are coming home." Tracey's face was red from where Cameron had smacked her.

"You come over here double teaming me and expect me to go home with you?" Cameron snarled, "Yeah whatever I'm out." Cameron announced standing up and grabbing his keys not bothering to check on the unconscious woman lying on the floor.

Tracey jumped up and ran out the door behind him. Ananda stood at a much slower pace because her head was throbbing, she felt as if the room were spinning. She looked at the nude woman that still lay on the floor unmoving and felt no remorse for her. When the woman eventually came to she would be wondering what happened Ananda could only hope that she would take it as a sign to leave Cameron alone, but her gut told her that it probably wouldn't. Locking the door before closing it she made her way back down the stairs headed to the car to make sure that neither Cam nor Tray killed the other. Able to hear the duo long before she could reach Cameron's truck she could tell that the argument was steadily escalating.

"You slashed all of my tires you stupid hoe!"

"Don't be calling me a hoe. You are one to talk. You're the one over here continually playing with your little whore and I'm not having it!" Tracey threatened Cameron, "You bring your ass home and I mean it!"

Ananda tuned them out as she stood by Cameron's truck quietly as they hashed through their problems. Situations like this one are exactly why she preferred to stay single. You just could never be certain to what someone was up to, no matter how much you wanted to trust them. After her relationship with Braxton years ago, Malcolm was the first man that she had given permission to be close enough to even begin to entertain the idea of being in a relationship.

Noticing that the arguing had stopped Ananda walked closer to Tracey and Cameron to see what was going on.

"Y'all okay over there?"

"Yes." Tracey told her, "We called a tow truck to come and get Cameron's truck and tow it to the house. Once they get here we'll take you home in my car.

"Okay cool." Ananda didn't say anything other than that as they all waited in Tracey's Lexus for the tow truck to arrive. Tracey and Cameron were talking as if everything was good and they hadn't been full-out fighting in hand-to-hand combat no more than a half hour ago, but who was Ananda to say anything. She wasn't married and didn't know what it was like to be married, so she stayed out of married people's business and waited patiently until they took her home.

Eight

$\mathcal{M}$alcolm sat in Ananda's apartment waiting for her and Tracey to come back from their little excursion. He wasn't sure where they went, but he knew it had to be serious to have them running out the house this time of night.

Looking down when his cell vibrated on his hip, he was instantly annoyed.

"What?" He listened to Merci for a second. "I don't have time for this unless something is wrong with Caprice, if not I have to go." He paused to hear what Merci had to say, "Where are you now? Okay. I'll be there in three hours. Look, that's the best I can do, you know I'm out the state right now. I'll be there. Let my angel know that I am coming."

"Hey." Ananda said to Malcolm as she came through the door of her place and caught him placing his cell phone in his pocket.

"Hey. You get everything straight with Tracey?"

"Yeah. She's as good as she's going to be. What about you? You okay?"

"I'm good."

"I'm sorry that I had to leave you like that." Ananda pulled Malcolm in close to her, what can I do to make it up to you?"

"You can--" A knock on the door interrupted Malcolm's sentence.

Ananda pulled away from Malcolm and walked toward the door. She knew it wasn't Tracey because she had a key and she and Cameron were headed home to work on them. Ananda wondered who would be knocking on her door this late. Putting her head up against the door to look through the peephole she was surprised to see a woman holding a child in her arms and another one standing beside her on the other side.

"Who is it?" Ananda called out. The woman's face wasn't facing forward toward the peephole so Ananda couldn't tell if it were someone she knew or not, but all of her friends knew not to show up unannounced at her place.

"Open the door it's Merci. Tell Malcolm to bring his ass out here this second!" The woman yelled.

Ananda glanced toward Malcolm who was standing in the middle of her floor looking like a deer caught in headlights as he moved toward the door.

"Friend of yours I take it?" Ananda asked sarcastically wondering why a woman was banging on her door this hour of night asking for Malcolm who wasn't even from this area.

Opening the door before Malcolm had a chance to reach it Ananda stared the woman up and down.

"Didn't your mother teach you manners? Because mine did and I know better than to knock on a stranger's door at this hour, or a stranger's door period."

"Oh please!" Merci said with attitude apparent in her tone and a sleeping Caprice in her arms and her ten-year-old daughter Tatiana beside her. "I could give two shits about you and what manners you have. Where is my daughter's father?" Merci attempted to step past Ananda, but Ananda blocked her path.

"You got me confused. I didn't invite you in. Try to walk past me again and you will be missing a leg." Ananda's expression read try me if you want to, she was already tired from having to ride out with Tracey. She didn't need this nonsense right now.

Merci arched her eyebrow as she took Ananda in welcoming the challenge, telling Tatiana to sit on the floor and gently placing a sleeping Caprice in her lap Merci attempted to push past Ananda again and against Ananda's better judgment she punched Merci in the mouth. She just wasn't in the mood for games tonight.

"I see you taking me for a joke." She exclaimed as she ducked away from Merci's punch and threw another one of her own connecting with Merci's jaw and listening to her scream in pain as blood flew out her mouth. "I'm not playing with you." Ananda screamed as she drew her arm back to hit Merci again, but was lifted from behind and placed inside her apartment. Malcolm went back into the hall and took Caprice out of Tatiana's arms telling her to stand up and follow him; he turned around to place Caprice in Ananda's arms before going back in the hall to speak to Merci locking the door behind him.

"You better get my daughters out of that apartment with that bitch!" Merci yelled from the hall as she kicked the door with all her might.

"Shorty you need to calm down." Malcolm pulled her away from the door as he tried to reason with her.

"I don't need to do a damn thing!" Merci screamed, "Get my babies out here right now."

"I swear I will leave you out here by yourself if you don't get it together." Malcolm said in a low calm tone as he forced himself to remain calm; trying his best not to go off on Merci himself. "What are you even doing here?"

"You think you just going to be out her doing whatever you want to do huh?!" Merci screamed. "We are a family." She said holding up her left hand with her engagement ring on it. "You, me, Tatiana and Caprice." Her voice escalating even more, she not caring who heard her or how crazy she appeared to be, "I've been with you for over ten years and you're out here doing God knows what with this tramp."

"She's not a tramp and you need to lower your voice."

"You get my babies out of there right now!" Merci screamed kicking the door again.

Inside the apartment Ananda, led Tatiana down the hall to her room and lay a sleeping Caprice onto her bed surrounding her with pillows in case she tried to roll. Ananda didn't want her falling onto the floor. "Will you be okay in here?" She asked Tatiana. The little girl nodded yes. Satisfied that the two little ones were comfortable, Ananda went back to the front of the apartment and opened the door.

"Kick my door one more time, just once more and see what happens." Ananda stared at Merci daring her with malice in her eyes.

"Oh, so you think that this is a game." Merci screamed while Malcolm held her back. Staring Ananda in her eyes Merci reared back and hock spit in her face narrowly missing her eye.

Ananda lunged at Merci as she felt the spit run down her face not giving a care that Malcolm was in between the two of them. She hit the two of them with enough force to send all three of them landing on the floor in a big heap. Ananda proceeded to punch what she could of Merci, her fists continually landing on her face. Merci feeling her eye begin to puff up wasn't one to take anything lightly; she was at a disadvantage with Malcolm's weight on top of her, but she still managed for her fist to connect with Ananda's mouth.

Ananda tasted blood as her lip split under the pressure of Merci's punch. Mad that the wench had been able to draw blood, Ananda's punches intensified.

Malcolm, stuck in the middle on the floor between the two battling women couldn't help but be assaulted by both women's barrage of punches. Untangling himself and standing up in the midst of their chaos on the floor; the two determined to beat each other to a pulp he grabbed Ananda who was on top and pulled her off of Merci.

"Let me go!" Ananda yelled as she kept kicking at Merci, "She think she gonna come to my place and disrespect me! No Sir! I am not having it! Not today!" Ananda kept attempting to push Malcolm off of her. "Move!"

Merci rolled to her feet while Malcolm had a good grip on Ananda, as she did she observed one of Ananda's neighbor's watching them through a crack in her door. "Mind your business!" Merci screamed as she took her shoe off and threw it at the door of the woman down the hall.

"I called the cops." The older woman said before firmly shutting the door.

"Fuck the cops!" Merci ranted.

Ananda kicked her legs out again at Merci, while Malcolm still had her in a vise grip and smiled as Merci hollered out in pain and buckled back to the floor when Ananda's foot connected with her shin.

"Yo shorty calm down." Malcolm spoke harshly to Ananda as he let her go to bend down and make sure that Merci was okay. Reaching his hands to her leg he was going to try and help her ease the pain. Even though they were no longer in a relationship and she was dead wrong for pulling a pop up with his daughter in tow, he didn't necessarily want bad things to happen to her and he still cared about her wellbeing.

Merci pushed his hands away and stood up awkwardly, flinching from the pain. "Don't you touch me. You'll never touch me again! I'm sick of this." She narrowed her eyes at Ananda attempting to take advantage of Malcolm being bent on the floor by swinging on her with all the strength she could muster up.

"That's enough Miss." Merci heard as she was roughly pushed up against the wall and cuffed by an officer that showed up at the precise time that she'd swung on Ananda.

"What is going on here?" Another officer asked Malcolm and Ananda.

"This crazy woman showed up on my doorstep and attacked me." Ananda responded before Malcolm had a chance to.

"So you're the one that lives here and you have no idea who this woman is?" The officer inquired.

"Yes, that is correct. Before she showed up on my doorstep unexpectedly, I had no idea who she was."

"Why aren't you asking me any questions?" Merci interrupted them with an attitude.

"Please be quiet ma'am. We will get to you when we take you down to the station."

Merci was in shock, "You're not taking her down to the station as well?"

"Ma'am an eye witness says you showed up at the scene and attacked the woman that lives here. We count that as assault ma'am and you are going down to the station alone."

Merci was livid and her temperament only escalated when she saw the nosey neighbor up the hall peeking out the crack of her door again. Merci narrowed her eyes and mouthed the words *You'll be sorry* to the older woman who promptly shut the door with a hard snap.

Later that evening after the police had left with Merci in tow Ananda lay on the sofa in her living room treating her swollen lip with ice.

"What's on your mind?" Malcolm asked her as he noticed how quiet she was being now that things had calmed down a bit and Merci was gone with the officers to the station.

"I'm obviously upset with you and how this whole evening went down. The first time you visit me and your crazy, trifling baby mama pops up from another state with your baby with her. I mean who does that but a psychotic B that's who." Ananda looked at Malcolm as if he had two heads. "Are you crazy, giving that chick my address!" She accused him. "You are a piece of work." she eyed him with disdain wanting to knock his head off. The only reason she had allowed him back into her apartment in the first place is because the girls were sleeping peacefully and Ananda didn't want anything else disturbing them. It was bad enough their mother had made them hop a plane to pull a pop up at another woman's place. The poor babies had endured a long enough day no thanks to their foolish parents.

Malcolm looked at Ananda as if *she* were crazy. "I would never do anything foul like give out your address. What kind of man do you think I am?" He shrugged his shoulders offended that she would think so lowly of him. "When Merci wants to know something she's good at finding out the answers she seeks."

"You have a whole lot of crazy that revolves around you and I don't want to be a part of it." Ananda was extremely upset by the recent events, "Do you know the last time I've been in an all out fight?" She asked him as the ice she was holding to her lip began to make her face numb, making her more irritated as he sat there quietly, staring at her not bothering to answer her question. "Not for years." She said answering her own question, "And I've never had someone bring an unwarranted fight to my front door." She spoke in a fierce whisper not wanting to wake the girls still fast asleep in her bedroom.

Malcolm knew that Ananda was mad at him and he couldn't say that he blamed her. He'd had no idea that Merci was going to pull the stunt that she did today.

"I'm truly sorry. I didn't mean to bring this foolishness to your doorstep. Please forgive me." Malcolm said to her sincerely. "What can I do to make this up to you? Because you're right my first time visiting you has been a complete disaster."

Ananda just looked at him no longer impressed and not wanting to be bothered any further.

"I'm not sure if this is something that you can make up. It has undoubtedly been a very long night; my body is in pain I wasn't anticipating an altercation this evening."

"I can fix this." Malcolm persisted. "And you're going to allow me that." Malcolm told her as he stood up.

Ananda narrowed her eyes not a fan of someone telling her what she was and wasn't going to do. "Oh really?" She questioned him.

"Yes, just give me a couple of minutes." He said as he headed toward the guest bathroom.

Ananda shrugged not feeling Malcolm at the moment. She could care less what he was up to. She had her mind made up. This was exactly the reason why she chose to remain single, between having to deal with Tracey and Cameron's drama earlier and now Malcolm and his daughter's mother they had all but solidified her resolve to remain alone.

Hearing the water running in the bathroom, Ananda wondered what Malcolm was up to. Maybe he felt like he was the stressed out one and needed to relax with a bath. For the life of her she couldn't understand what he had to be stressed about.

Malcolm strutted back into the living room ten minutes later where Ananda was laid across the sofa in a deep slumber. Leaning down Malcolm gently lifted her into his arms and carried her into the bathroom. Bending his head slightly to graze hers he carefully nudged her awake.

"Mmmmm." Ananda mumbled lowly not wanting to open her eyes.

"Wake up sleepy head." Malcolm said softly. "I have a surprise for you."

"Too tired for a surprise." Ananda mumbled still not cooperating.

"Please Ananda open your eyes." Malcolm requested patiently.

"Fine." Ananda snapped grumpily as she opened her eyes since he refused to let her sleep. Her face registered one of shock when she realized what he had done. The entire guest bathroom was illuminated with tea lit scented candles. The bathtub was filled to the brim with bubbles and he had her silk pink robe hanging on the hook behind the door.

"What in the world?" She whispered fully awake at this point glancing up at Malcolm.

Malcolm smiled down at her, this is me attempting to make tonight up to you."

Ananda didn't return his smile. "I already told you that I don't believe you can make this up, but this is a good start I must say."

"Good." Malcolm replied placing her feet on the floor. "Get undressed and in the tub, I'll be back to bathe you in two minutes."

Ananda watched as Malcolm turned and walked out the bathroom in a polite courteous attempt to respect her privacy. Swiftly removing her clothes, she eased herself into the hot bubbly water and felt her body begin to relax immediately. She couldn't even lie to herself after the chaotic evening she'd had, this is exactly what the doctor had ordered.

Malcolm reentered the bathroom in exactly two minutes. Kneeling down so that he could be level with the bathtub he looked deep into her eyes.

"I apologize for what happened earlier tonight and I mean that." He gingerly placed his hands in Ananda's bath water. She eyed him warily until she felt his fingers wrap around her foot and began to knead them slowly. "Let me show you how much." He said in a husky whisper.

Ananda wasn't in a position to deny him anything at the moment. Her body was bruised from her altercations earlier that evening. Her head hurt from when it hit the ground, her hand hurt from punching Merci and she had a split lip, a massage was heaven sent and very welcome. Her body was silently rejoicing.

"Okay." She whispered back, "You can show me." Resting her head on the back of the bathtub Ananda closed her eyes and let Malcolm work his magic and massage every inch of her body in the water.

Malcolm was thoroughly enjoying rubbing Ananda's body, so he didn't mind the silence as she allowed his hands to roam freely. When he heard her breath begin to even he realized that she had fallen asleep. Careful not to wake her he picked up the soap before the water cooled too much and began bathing her body.

When Malcolm was done bathing Ananda he pulled a clean plush navy blue towel from her towel rack and gently pushed her short curly hair off of her face. Noticing how full her lips appeared, no doubt due to the cut she had he figured it was now or never as he leaned down for a kiss convincing himself that that would be the most effective way to wake her up. Careful not to apply to much pressure because of her bruised mouth he lightly brushed his lips against hers.

Ananda's eyes fluttered open when Malcolm's lips made contact with hers and she stared directly into his apprehensive ones while he held his breath waiting for her reaction.

Ananda felt herself instantly become turned on, it had been so long since she'd has this much contact with a man. Not trusting herself she sat up abruptly breaking all contact with Malcolm, their stolen moment broken.

"Can you hand me a towel please?" Ananda asked as she shivered from the cool water or maybe it was the intensity of his gaze she wasn't sure which.

Malcolm stared into Ananda's eyes a moment longer before handing the towel to her and turning his back so that she could get out of the bathtub without him gawking at her.

"I'm decent." He turned back around to face her and marveled at how striking she looked with her wet hair wrapped in a towel and no makeup.

"Why are you staring at me like that?"

"I was thinking about how good you look." Malcolm told her as a light bulb went off in his head. "Get dressed." He said abruptly, "I want to talk to you about something important."

Ananda looked at him skeptically wondering what important thing he had to say to her. "Thank you for the bath and the massage." She said as she brushed past him to quietly enter her room. Loath to cut the light on to avoid disturbing the girls Ananda felt around her room in the dark until she reached the opening of her walk in closet.

Closing the closet door behind her she found the dangling light string and pulled until her closet brightened as if the sun were in the room. Taking in the mess in her closet, she shook her head. There were clothes thrown everywhere and she began to wonder what she should put on. Not owning a decent pair of pajamas because she preferred to sleep without any clothes on she was stumped. She wanted to put on something that was semi sexy giving a little but not too much because she was still angry with him about the foolishness she'd had to endure. Finally deciding on a white tank top and white cotton shorts with nothing underneath and bare feet, she cut the light off in the closet and quietly made her way back to the living room to join Malcolm.

When Ananda entered the living room Malcolm took in her tight white top that visibly displayed her hard nipples and her white cotton shorts that he would swear in any courtroom if they called him to testify; were telling him to take them off and almost lost his focus. Noticing her red toe nail polish on her bare feet for the first time and the way that she was looking at him now only confirmed that he was making the right decision.

"What's up?" Ananda asked him as she sat in the chair across from the sofa and curled her legs beneath her. She wondered if he were paying attention to the time. She felt as if this were the longest night of her life.

"I know you're on the fence about me personally right now, but I have a business proposition for you if you're interested."

Ananda remained silent as he continued. "There has recently been a new model casting call that I heard about and I was wondering if you may be interested. I believe you have the look they are going for and it you were to land the job it would be for a national campaign." He eyed her inquiringly. "What do you think?"

Ananda was dumbfounded her sleepiness melting away, "A national campaign? You think I have what it takes to be part of a national campaign?" She asked excitedly.

"I do." Malcolm replied earnestly as he watched her animated face. He paused before continuing. "Does that look of glee mean you'll finally forgive me for earlier and we can start over?"

"Yes!" Ananda exclaimed, "This makes up for everything." She leapt out the chair and enfolded him into a giant hug.

"You're amazing." She was so happy that she could barely contain herself her excitement at the prospect of having more money in her bank account to help pay her bills.

"I'm glad you're so appreciative." Malcolm told her as he returned her hug.

"What all do I have to do?" Ananda asked releasing him, but remaining close to his side.

"For starters, you'll attend a party with me in two weeks. It'll be in D.C. and it's hosted by the agency conducting the talent search."

"Perfect!" Ananda responded calmly when she really wanted to scream to the heavens. "I will definitely be ready, with everything but bells on."

Malcolm smiled at her, "Good, I look forward to it."

$\mathscr{N}$ine

$\mathscr{H}$unter maintained his cool as he strutted into the Grand Hyatt Hotel in downtown D.C.; secretly impressed with the outcome of the networking event that Lorna had diligently planned for the agency.

"Mr. Lewis, I'm so glad that you've arrived." Lorna gushed as she anxiously greeted him. She knew that she had done an amazing job on this event and could barely contain her own excitement.

Hunter thought that Lorna looked beautiful as he took in her body hugging electric blue dress, her plunging neckline that showed off her full bust size and made a mental note to speak with her about her appearance. Even though she looked good Hunter had a standard for his employees and he felt that Lorna was not displaying the level of professionalism that he wanted attached to his company's brand.

"You've done an amazing job." Hunter praised her as he took in the large number of A-list clientele in attendance at the event.

"Follow me. There is a very important person that has been waiting to meet you." Lorna led Hunter to the V.I.P. lounge past security stopping only once before they reached a distinguished gentleman.

"Mr. Walters, this is Hunter Lewis. Mr. Lewis, Malcolm Walters." Lorna introduced the two men before stepping away to check on a problem with security she saw in the back of the room. "Excuse me gentlemen."

"It is nice to meet you." Malcolm said extending his hand out to shake Hunter's. Hunter took his hand and smiled warmly at the man.

"Likewise Mr. Walters," Hunter replied, "I hear that you are doing some exciting things in Atlanta to increase the visibility of the city's up and coming lifestyle and cultural activities within the African American community." Malcolm nodded, "I respect that."

Malcolm nodded at Hunter again not feeling especially respected as Hunter gazed over his shoulder appearing to be in search of a more meaningful conversation. Even though they hadn't exchanged many words to one another, Malcolm felt as if Hunter was speaking down to him and being dismissive.

"Thank you. There is a young lady that I believe you should meet." Malcolm stated just as Hunter's assistant Lorna came back over.

"Excuse me Mr. Lewis, but the Mayor is here and he is requesting your presence."

"Thank you Lorna." Hunter said before glancing back to Malcolm. "Malcolm, again, it was nice meeting you. Please enjoy the party and find me before you leave." Hunter said as he returned his attention to Lorna who led him to where the District's Mayor was waiting. Ananda took in her extravagant surroundings. She had never been at an upscale event such as this one. The ballroom was large by any man's standards. The low lighting and red up-lighting gave the room an intimate, sexy feel. Ananda was drawn to the bar area where there was a human sized ice luge with the letters L.T.A.M. standing for Lyric Talent Agency and Marketing engraved on the front. She was enthralled.

Malcolm didn't know what to make of his meeting of Hunter but he was elated to have Ananda on his arm at the party where Hunter was launching the official casting call for the national campaign. By the tell-tale signs on the faces of all the men looking on as he and Ananda walked by, Malcolm knew that he was the envy of every man in the exquisite ballroom.

He was trying to find a way to introduce her to Hunter. The man didn't seem to know the meaning of finding one spot and staying in it.

"Oh… my… gosh!" Ananda practically yelled to be heard over the music, "It's Oprah! He knows Oprah! This is craziness" she said   excitedly.

Malcolm gazed into her eyes and smiled happy that she was happy.

Ananda had never imagined a world quite like this one. Glancing down at her gown she felt as if she were a part of a fairy tale. When Malcolm had arrived to pick her up she'd been clothed in a cute little party dress that she'd picked up from Macy's on her way home from work the previous day. Malcolm had taken one look at her, told her that she was beautiful and promptly had the driver take then to Neiman Marcus on Wisconsin Avenue to find her the beautiful Michael Kors gown that she was draped in right now. The dress accentuated her curves and was a Bryant red. He also allowed her to purchase black peep-toe red bottoms. She'd been elated, never in her life had she worn clothes like this or been in the presence of so many fabulous people at one time. She was having the night of her life.

As Ananda gazed around the lavish ballroom with hanging crystals adorning the ceiling, her eyes briefly connected with the man Malcolm had spoken with when they'd first entered the ballroom. She'd been too captivated by her surroundings to pay attention to him at the time, but now with no distraction she became blatantly aware of how handsome he was. Breaking eye contact before she reacted under his magnetic stare she focused on Malcolm who was taking painstaking care to introduce her to any and everybody at the event.

"Are you enjoying yourself?" Malcolm asked her as they walked away from the Editor-in-Chief of Essence magazine.

"I am immensely." Ananda beamed back at him. They had been at the event for a little over two hours now and all the wine was making her bladder angry with her. "I'm going to run to the ladies room." She told him as she gently touched his arm.

"Okay, hurry back."

"I will." She told him as she scurried out the doors of the ballroom to locate the restroom.

When Ananda exited the ladies room a man was stationed on the wall across from the door as if he were waiting for someone. It was the enigmatic stranger that she had caught eyeing her throughout the whole evening.

"Hello." Ananda nodded her head at the host of the event who's deep brown chestnut eyes were gazing longingly into hers, as she attempted to side step him to reenter the ballroom, but proved too quick for her and swiftly blocked her path forcing her to back up into a corner.

"I only want one moment of your time." Hunter spoke calmly not wanting her to bolt away from him. He could tell by her demeanor and the unwelcome look in her eyes that she didn't appreciate him holding her captive.

"Yes, how may I help you?" Ananda politely asked him. She was trying to remain gracious to her host but didn't take kindly to being ambushed while she made a quick dash to the ladies room.

"I've been looking for an opportunity to introduce myself to you all evening." Hunter began.

Ananda lifted her eyebrow but remained silent. Even though the host of the evening came off as creepy and lurking in hallways, he did have the right connections that she needed in order to pursue a career in modeling and after all meeting him was the reason she was at the event in the first place. So even if she had to bite her tongue she was going to be nice to him.

"I'm Hunter Lewis, the host of this event." He told her as he held out his hand.

Ananda extended her hand as well, thinking it the appropriate thing to do. Hunter enclosed her tiny hand in his and held it a moment longer than necessary and she told him her name was Ananda.

"A beautiful name for a beautiful woman." He brought her hand to his lips and placed a light kiss.

Ananda gazed at him unimpressed. She hated men like this; so full of themselves they couldn't see straight and Hunter, she could tell, was very full of himself.

"It is a pleasure to meet you." She told him as she retracted her hand from his firm grip. "I apologize, Mr. Lewis, but I'm sure my date for the evening will be searching for me. I really must return inside." Ananda was doing her best to rush the conversation.

"Of course." Hunter told her as he pulled out a business card and handed it to her. "You have a look that I believe I can market, why not give me a call Monday morning to schedule a time you can come in for some test shots.

"There you are." A woman dressed in blue exclaimed as she burst out the doors of the ballroom before Ananda had a chance to answer. The woman narrowed her eyes at Ananda as she slid it between the two of them.

"Lorna," Hunter began not wanting to appear rude, "this is Ananda."

Lorna fixed a dazzling smile on her face as she turned around to formally meet the beautiful woman in red that have been occupying Mr. Lewis' time.

"It is a pleasure to meet you." Lorna said to the woman.

Ananda gazed at the woman in the expensive dress displaying a smile that didn't reach her eyes and noticed she did not extend her hand for Ananda to shake, which was customary when being introduced to someone.

"The pleasure is yours." Ananda responded smiling genuinely at the woman but wanting her to know that she wasn't buying her attempt at trying to be nice. She knew a problem when she saw one and this woman would definitely be one.

"Lorna," Hunter spoke breaking the uncomfortable silence, "Ananda will be calling the office Monday morning" he glanced at Ananda, "hopefully to make arrangements to come in for test shots. When she calls be sure to put her straight through to me directly."

Ananda noticed that he said when and not if she called.

"Of course, Mr. Lewis," Lorna said as she turned back to face him, "I hate to interrupt you, but there is something inside that requires your attention. Please excuse us Ananda." She offered as she took Hunter's arm not looking back in Ananda's direction as she led him back into the ballroom.

When they opened the doors to go inside, Ananda saw Malcolm step out. "Are you doing okay out here?" He asked her, "thought you may have gotten lost or worse came to your senses and left me here alone.

Ananda smiled, grateful that he had come to find her. "Neither just got tied up speaking with Hunter Lewis, who gave me his business card and asked me to call him on Monday morning to schedule a time to come in for some test shots." Ananda handed Malcolm the card that was still in her hand.

"That's great!" Malcolm exclaimed picking her up and twirling her around. "We'll call first thing Monday morning."

"We?" Ananda arched an eyebrow.

"Absolutely, as your manager it's my job to be available to take calls for my client."

"So, I'm your client now?" Ananda asked in a serious tone purposely giving Malcolm a hard time.

Malcolm scooped her up, "We'll work out the many details later."

"Alright." Ananda looked up at him, "There are some other details that I want to work out as well." She eyed him up and down, "You ready to leave or do we need to stay?" She asked him.

"The way you're looking in that dress, I'd say that we can definitely leave, especially since you've already met Mr. Lewis – mission accomplished!

"Good. That's what I wanted to hear. Let's go." Ananda told him.

On the way back to Ananda's apartment the two couldn't keep their hands off one another. Ananda allowed Malcolm to run his fingers up and down the length of her body. She knew that he's wanted to touch her this way since the moment they met. When the car arrived at Ananda's high-rise apartment building things in the back seat were getting hot and heavy. By the time the two reached Ananda's apartment door she could barely stick the key into the lock before Malcolm him was reconnected to her body.

Body limbs entangled up in one another Malcolm somehow managed to push the door closed with his foot and drag Ananda to the floor with him. There was no way they were going to make it to her bedroom. He had to know how she tasted, the raging need and intense anticipation was starting to get the best of him. Ever since she emerged from Neiman's dressing room in the brilliant red dress he has been fantasizing about getting underneath it. For the next two hours the sound of lovemaking could be heard coming from Ananda's apartment. Later that evening Malcolm kissed her forehead as she snuggled in his arms. Ananda kept her eyes shut when Malcolm's lips grazed the spot above her eyes.

Resting peacefully, this is the most content I've ever been. She thought to herself.

Ten

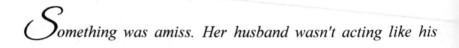

Something was amiss. Her husband wasn't acting like his normal self. She'd tried talking to him about it but he kept saying that everything was fine, but she knew for a fact that everything was not fine. He was beginning to slack on his husbandly duties, the husbandly duties that she had become accustomed to every night. She didn't know everything, but she knew without a doubt that something in the water wasn't clean. She had never suspected him of anything before but if he was creeping around with another woman she was going to find out about it and everyone would feel her wrath.

Eleven

"Are you hungry?" Merci asked as she placed a plate of cheese pizza in front of Caprice and Tatiana at the table.

Malcolm shook his head no turning up the volume to the 50' flat screen LED TV that he had mounted on the wall. He and Merci had settled their differences after the stunt she had pulled by popping up at Ananda's apartment that resulted in her getting locked up, but not before the next incident where she popped up at a restaurant and started yet another fight with Ananda. Malcolm had had to talk fast to get Merci to understand that their current situation could stay as it was. He agreed to be more mindful of her feelings, but he also made it clear that she needed to respect his space and not to involve his daughter in anymore of her foolishness.

Looking down as his phone vibrated Malcolm stood and retreated to the bathroom.

"Hey babe," he says speaking softly into the receiver.

"Are you coming by tonight?" The caller asked.

"No, I won't be able to make it out there tonight." He then added before hanging up, "I apologize."

Opening the bathroom door, he jumped back a little in shock to see Merci standing there with an attitude tapping her foot.

"Who was that?" She asked him. "Since when do you have to go into the bathroom to take a call?"

"Since about the time you decided to become *"inch high, private eye."* Malcolm said to her candidly.

Merci narrowed her eyes. "You keep playing with me and I swear you will regret it."

Malcolm pushed past Merci with an air of indifference. He didn't feel like playing any games with her today.

"Please kill the attitude. I'm not in the mood for your mess today." He told her calmly as he walked back to the sofa to finish watching the basketball game. The Hawks were playing the Wizards in Atlanta. Right now the Wizards have possession of the ball, power forward Cameron Miller drives the ball up the lane for an easy layup off the glass. Malcolm cursed under his breath. He had bet $4000 on the Hawks winning and right now they were down 83 - 119 with two minutes left in the fourth quarter. Shaking his head in disgust as the Hawk's Jamal Crawford misses a must have shot from the top of the key -- he kisses his money goodbye.

"Damn." He mumbled.

"What's wrong daddy?" Caprice's high-pitched voice inquired from the table where her fingers and face were practically covered in tomato sauce from the pizza that she was eating.

"Nothing Princess," Malcolm responded gently, "finish your pizza."

"Okay daddy." She said happily as she licked her fingers and returning to the task of demolishing her pizza.

"I wasn't done talking to you." Merci's annoyed voice said lowly from behind him. Malcolm sighed as he turned to face her.

"I'm done." He said to her as he went to the hall closet and grabbed his hat. "I'll be back later." He opened the door and left without looking back in her direction. Her nagging him every two seconds was making him agitated, so he needed a change of scenery. Pulling up to his favorite sports bar, Dantanna's over on Lenox Road, he just needed some time to unwind without being bothered by anyone.

"Can I get a shot of Petron, and a vodka and cranberry please?" He told the bartender, "Let me have the shot first." He took a seat on the barstool scanning the monitors scattered about the room waiting to see which contest would catch his interest.

Malcolm turned his head toward the commotion rising near the front door of the bar. Camera flashes and cell phones are directed and at the ready. It's probably some ATL reality star and their publicists creating a staged "sighting" or something, he mused to himself. People sure can get into an uproar about the most fake and insignificant crap. As the crowd shifted he was able to see Cameron Miller and John Wall enter into the bar with two sexy women walking with them. As they came toward the bar, Malcolm recognized one of the women.

"Tracey?" Malcolm said without thinking twice.

Conversation between the two men ceased as Cameron focused his undivided attention on Malcolm.

"How do you know my wife?" Cameron asked stepping close to Malcolm; a tense expression on his face and John Wall stepping closer as well. Malcolm immediately stood up willing to meet the imposing threat head on.

"Cam calm down." Tracey said quickly as she grabbed Cameron's arm. "This is Ananda's boo Malcolm. Remember, I was telling you about him?"

Cameron relaxed immediately, then holding out his hand to shake Malcolm's, "Yo, my bad. Didn't know who was shouting my wife's name out like they knew her. Not looking for problems man."

Malcolm took his hand, "no problem. Good to meet you bro'. The game tonight, man you cost me four grand."

"You bet on the wrong team then." Cameron smirked as he withdrew his hand from Malcolm and pulled his wife in close by the waist.

"You can join us if you want. Ananda's cool peoples with me, so you good." Cameron offered him.

"That's okay. Thanks for the offer; I'm gonna split in a minute." Malcolm told him.

"Cool." Cameron dapped him up, "make sure you bet on the right team next time."

Malcolm smiled as their small group walked away to a private table. Huh, he would never bet on the Wizards he thought to himself. They just happened to have a lucky night. Shaking his head, he chuckled to himself, paid his tab and headed back to the house and his complicated life with Merci and the girls.

***

"Did you call him yet?" Malcolm asked into the phone receiver.

"No. I'm going to reach out to him after you and I get off the phone."

"Why are you waiting? Do you want me to make the call for you?" Malcolm asked her.

"No." Ananda told him indignantly, "If you do that he'll think I can't take care of my own affairs. I got this."

"Okay. Just know I'm here if you need me."

"I know you are and I appreciate that." Ananda took a small pause before asking hesitantly, "What are you up to this weekend? How would you feel about me coming down to visit? A change of scenery would be nice." She added with a lilt to her voice, trying not to sound nervous.

Malcolm caught off guard by her question tried to run all the pros and cons through his mind as fast as he could.

Ananda waited fretfully for him to answer. The longer he was silent the more she began to wonder if it was a good idea to suggest that she come down to visit first without waiting for him to invite her.

"Uh, I guess that will be okay." Malcolm heard himself say feeling as if he were experiencing an out of body experience.

"Why you say it like that? Do you want me to come or don't you?" she said sassily. She was starting to relax at his accepting her proposal.

"I definitely want you to come." Malcolm told her, "and I mean that in every sense of the word."

Ananda blushed thinking about the night of passionate lovemaking that he had put on her body. "Oh really?" She flirted back with him in a husky sexually charged tone.

Malcolm could already feel his crotch responding to the subtle implication of her reply. "I wish you were here right now so that you can see what you're doing to me."

Ananda chuckled seductively into the phone. "Don't worry I'll be there soon enough."

"Can't wait." He told her, then refocusing on the matter at hand, "Now back to business, make that call to Hunter Lewis and let's make it happen, baby ."

"Yes Sir." Ananda laughed hanging up the phone.

Twelve

"*M*r. Lewis, you have a call on line one." Lorna announced to Hunter through the intercom.

"Thank you. Hunter Lewis here."

"Hello Mr. Lewis, you may not remember me but my name is Ananda. We met at your networking event over the weekend and you handed me your business card.

Hunter leaned back in his chair and propped his feet on his desk and crossed his long legs at the ankles. "Ananda, of course I remember you. I'm glad you made it your business to call me. I trust you know that is a very wise first move."

Ananda had to choke back a sarcastic reply. What a pompous ass! She thought to herself, It's funny what good looks, power and a little money will do to people. It made her sick to her stomach, but if he could help further her modeling career, she'll just have to look past his arrogance.

"Is that right?" She said, mindful of her tone.

"That was very right indeed." Hunter responded, "The second right thing you did was ensuring that you nabbed the attention of the CEO of an up and coming talent agency. So kudos to you on that savvy move as well." Hunter chuckled into the phone.

It took everything in Ananda not to hang up the phone. She thought, "Great physical package, but no prize inside, ugh!"

"I find that very interesting." Ananda added quickly since he appeared to be waiting for an appreciative response to what he obviously considered a brilliant insight.

"You know what I find interesting Ananda?"

"No. What?" She asked, continuing with the charade.

"That today's your lucky day. I am currently working on a campaign for Colgate that will be shown nationally and I would like you to fly up to New York and do some tests shots for me. Let's say tomorrow. Are you available?"

Ananda worked a nine to five and knew she wouldn't be able to take off with such short notice.

"I'm not sure if that will work. I can't just take off from my job like that." Ananda began.

"Ananda, how many times have you pretty much been handed a deal? I'm offering you the opportunity of a lifetime. Do you have any idea of how many women would kill to be in your position? Say yes and worry about the rest later. After tomorrow you will never need another *job* ever again."

Ananda thought about it for second and he is right she told herself. I am today's discovery; there is another pretty young woman that could be in his face by lunch time. He is making sense, this is my chance. Calling him was a good move; capturing his attention was another. He is offering me a shot at a world-wide career and I'm thinking about some piddling nine-to-five job.

"Ooookay." Ananda dragging the word out, barely able to breathe. "You're right. I'll call out sick and come up there for the photo shoot."

"Wonderful. That's what I like to hear. I'll put my assistant Lorna back on the line to gather a few details from you so we can book your flight in the morning. I look forward to seeing you then." Hunter placed her on hold and buzzed Lorna.

"Yes Mr. Lewis."

"Ananda is holding on the line to talk with you, book her on an early flight to New York and set up the itinerary for her photo shoot. Thank you."

****

Ananda arrived at JFK airport at 6:45 in the morning. Hunter's assistant Lorna had booked her on a 5:45 AM flight out of National. She didn't know if she were being punked or punished; it is way too early to be up and traveling anywhere.

Ananda was thankful that Tracey was able to make the last minute trip with her so that she wouldn't have to travel alone.

"How are you feeling?" Tracey asked as they walked to where the cars would be waiting.

"I'm tired, but excited." Ananda gave a little smile and that was the truth. She was very excited about the shoot and for a national campaign! She had never done anything like this in her life. She is still processing how this is happening to her.

"I'm sooooo excited for you." Tracey exclaimed as they headed outside to where a car was waiting for them.

"There's your name." Tracey said pointing to a driver holding a sign with her name in big black letters, standing in front of a black Lincoln town car. She quickly looked around to see if anyone noticed her star treatment. Unfortunately, this is not such a rare sight in the Big Apple. Oh well, it's a big deal to me! She thought with glee as she waived at the driver and he promptly came over to relieve both women of their burdensome luggage.

"I truly love all of this." Tracey couldn't help expressing her happiness as they made themselves comfortable inside the car. "While it's on my mind, did I tell you that I saw Malcolm when Cameron played in Atlanta over the weekend?"

"No, you didn't tell me." Ananda looked hard at her. It was so unlike Tracey not to call her immediately when something crazy or random strikes her as newsworthy. Seeing Malcolm again, especially after how he was introduced to her, most certainly meets the criteria for a call.

"Yeah. He was at this bar we went in after the game. He was all alone though."

"Okay. He never said anything to me about seeing you."

Tracey shrugged, "Guess he didn't figure it to be a big deal."

"Guess not." Ananda echoed as the driver pulled up to a building on a busy street in the city.

"I was told to direct you to go up to the fifth floor where someone will greet you and help you from there." The driver told them.

"Wonderful. Thank you." Ananda also thanked the doorman who held the beautiful brass lobby doors for her and Tracey.

Entering the magnificent glass building Ananda was impressed. As she stood in the grand lobby, she peered upward at an impressive atrium of modern light fixtures, which reflected and bounced off the glass, brass and steel trimmings much like sparkling crystal. She couldn't wait for an opportunity to see this place at nighttime.

She and Tracey took the elevator to the fifth floor and Ananda had to catch her breath once the elevator doors opened. The reception area was decorated with an eclectic collection of art work. She recognized what she surmised to be an original Salvador Dali. The surrealism of the office space was so stunning that Ananda was wary about touching anything for fear of breaking something or otherwise spoiling the sight. The carpet was a plush ebony color which provided the backdrop for white, ultra-modern, European furnishings. Definitely not IKEA! Ananda immediately made a beeline to what appeared to be the safest place to stand in the reception area and waited patiently for instructions.

Hunter had anticipated Ananda's arrival as her driver had phoned to say that he had already delivered her and a friend at the building.

"Hello again," he said as he approached the reception desk.

"Nice to see you again." Ananda told him.

"The pleasure is definitely mine." Hunter told her as he captured her hand in his and lifted it to his lips.

Ananda cringed on the inside, but made it a point not to display any emotion and breathed a sigh of relief when after releasing her hand turned and greeted Tracey likewise.

"I've not had the pleasure of meeting you. I see that beautiful women travel in packs. What's your name gorgeous?" Tracey gave him a look of amusement and then eyed Ananda hard with a look that said, is this guy for real? Ananda averted her gaze from Tracey's so as to avoid bursting into laughter in Hunter's presence.

"Tracey Miller." She told him stifling a laugh in the process.

"I'm Hunter Lewis and it's apparent that I am one lucky man today."

"Mr. Lewis," Ananda interrupted his attempts at chauvinism, "Where would you like me to go so we can get started?" She asked as the striking brunette that she recognized from the party made her way over to them to stand next to Hunter. Ananda was in a rush to get things moving along. She didn't come all the way to New York to stand in the lobby with some delusional man who believed himself to be god's personal gift to women.

"Please call me Hunter, I insist." He told her, "My assistant Lorna will show you where to go. I will see you in about an hour when it's time to get the photo shoot underway."

"Thank you, Mr. Lewis." Ananda responded politely wanting to make it clear to him that this was business and she would address him as such. They weren't friends to be on a first name basis. Hunter received her message loud and clear and left them in Lorna's care as he retreated to his office.

As soon as Hunter was out of vision and hearing range the smile disappeared from Lorna's face. She knew all too well who Ananda was and that apparently Hunter seemed to have a mild crush on her.

"Follow me." She told them with an obvious attitude.

Ananda and Tracey exchanged glances. "As long as she don't start nothing, there won't be nothing." Tracey whispered as they followed Lorna to the room for makeup and hair. Ananda giggled at Tracey's comment. "Right."

"Once your hair and makeup is done I will take you to the studio area where the photo shoot will be held." Lorna explained to them in an icy tone.

"Someone in this room needs to fix their attitude and I'm only going to say it once." Tracey spoke brashly. Ananda knew Tracey was a ticking time bomb, neither one of them took kindly to someone who didn't know the appropriate tone in which to speak to them.

"Tray, don't." Ananda shook her head, "Ignore her. I'm here for business okay. We don't want any problems."

Tracey stared Lorna down and Lorna stared back at her. "I know this is business but respect will be given."

"Tracey, let it go." Ananda told her as she sat in the chair where one slender man was waiting with a makeup cover to place over her clothes and another one had a blond wig in his hands.

"Not until she understands that I'm dead serious. Not playing with her."

Lorna looked Tracey up and down from head to toe and that was more than Tracey could take. Before Lorna or anyone knew what happened her head snapped sharply to the left from Tracey's smack that echoed through the room.

Ananda's eyes widen in horror as she quickly jumped out of her makeup chair.

"Tracey!"

"It wasn't my fault. The stupid witch looked me up and down." Tracey shrugged as if to say whatever.

Lorna stood there right cheek throbbing as she turned bright red from embarrassment and fled the room.

"Tracey you can't just walk around hitting people. This is a new business venture for me and I don't want you to jeopardize that by assaulting the staff!

"Honey, she deserved that." One of the slender men said snapping his fingers.

"Okay." Said the other one, "it's about time someone knocked the diva off her high horse and down a notch or two. Now sit on down here girl so you can get this hair makeup done."

"Don't worry about her." The first one spoke again, "she's harmless. Her ego is just bruised if anything."

"You sure?" Ananda asked as she hesitantly sat back into the hair and makeup chair, "this is a great opportunity for me and I don't want any problems."

"It'll be fine." The second man told her, "Now relax and let's go to work."

Ananda did as told and relaxed.

An hour later Hunter walked into hair and makeup to find Ananda completely transformed. Her short curly black hair gone replaced with a blond wavy Beyoncé like wig. Her makeup was very natural with her face radiant and gold tones and hues that made her naturally brown eyes pop.

"You look amazing." Hunter remarked as he gave her face a thorough review.

Ananda smiled a genuine smile at him because for once he sounded genuine and not full of self-absorption.

"Thank you," she said dramatically, "I'm all ready for my close-up."

"Yes you are." He added in a deep, serious voice; obviously playing along.

"Mr. Lewis they're ready for her on set."

Lorna announced popping back in at that moment eyes focused only on Hunter.

Tracey smirked from the observation but didn't comment, while Ananda made it her business to ignore Tracey.

"Please follow me." Lorna said to the group as she guided them to the studio.

Ananda stepped foot into the cold from and looked around a bit disappointed. This room wasn't as immaculate as the rest of the luxurious office. The room was chilly and was a definite contrast from the rest of the rooms they've seen so far. There was cloth covering the windows, the floor was stark white, there were cables, lights, carts and props littered all over the room. If it weren't for the upbeat attitude of the photographer this part of the trip would really have been a drag.

"Let's do this." The photographer announced once she stepped into the room. The photographer led her to a spot in the center of the floor and before she knew what was happening he was snapping away.

A few hours later all Ananda could remember about the shoot was lean this way, smile, not that hard, place your arm here, move your head like this. She was physically and mentally exhausted. Her entire body ached and while she did little other than observe, she could tell that Tracey was beat as well as they flew in total silence, back to National airport leaving her modeling future totally in the hands of Hunter Lewis.

Thirteen

$\mathcal{M}$alcolm was anxiously waiting at Hartsfield airport for

Ananda to come. He had to jump through quite a few hoops to make this weekend possible for the two of them. He'd told Merci that he was going to be out of town on business for the weekend and he truly hoped that was enough to keep her for trying to dig up some dirt.

Seeing her curly head, come through baggage claim Malcolm was instantly in a good mood. Smiling as she spotted him, he waved at her. Taking her bag when she was close enough to him he leaned down to give her a kiss.

"I've missed you." Ananda told him and she hugged him with all her might.

"I missed you more." Malcolm told her as they exited the airport and crossed the parking lot to his black Range Rover. "I got us a room at the Westin on Peachtree for the weekend."

"That's fine by me. Ananda told him.

"And we have dinner reservations at eight."

Ananda looked down at her crystal encased Michael Kors watch that read 7:30 p.m., "Good thing I came in looking semi-decent on the plane. I feel like this is a set up." She laughed.

"I think you are beautiful anyway that you come." Malcolm gave her a lazy smile as his voice deepened.

"Ok Mister, none of that stuff." Ananda laughed, "How are you trying to seduce me and we haven't even made it to dinner yet? These cookies ain't free."

"I didn't know paying a compliment was seducing."

"Mmmhmmn. You know what you're doing." She smiled mischievously, "And I kind of like it."

"Good, and there is lots more where that came from." Malcolm told her as her held open the truck door for her.

Once Malcolm was in the truck and they were headed toward their destination Ananda couldn't keep her excitement to herself.

"Guess who just booked a national ad campaign for Colgate?"

Malcolm took his eyes off the road to focus on Ananda's excited face for a moment before redirecting his attention back to the road. "Who?" He asked playing along with her, although he already knew. He'd received a call from Hunter himself letting his know that Malcolm's client had been booked.

"Me! Can you believe it?" Ananda exclaimed happily.

"Yes I absolutely can. Didn't I tell you that you definitely have what it takes?"

Ananda eyed him slyly, "Why yes you did kind sir. Seems like you may know a thing or two about what you speak." She said with a smile.

Out of his peripheral vision Malcolm could see her smiling at him, without taking his eyes off the road he smiled as well. "It would seem a celebration is in order and I chose just the place." He told her.

Malcolm took Ananda directly to the Bacchanalia. It is one of his favorite restaurants and is no more than ten minutes from the hotel.

"This is so nice." Ananda told him once they entered and were seated.

"Wait until you try the food." Malcolm told her.

"Hello sir, madam. May I take your drink orders please?"

Ananda was impressed; they hadn't been seated for more than a minute before the maître d' came to their table.

"Yes," Malcolm replied. "What type of wine do you like?" he asked Ananda.

"I love Moscato D'Asti" Ananda answered.

Malcolm looked at the maître d'. "Do you have that?"

"Yes sir. I will get for you."

"Thank you." Malcolm nodded his head.

"Thank you for bringing me out tonight." Ananda smiled.

"The pleasure is definitely mine. Trust me." Malcolm told her.

The maître d' arrived with the bottle of wine in an ice bucket that he sat on the table. Ananda watched as he took his corkscrew out of his apron and uncorked their bottle all in one fluid motion.

"Thank you." Malcolm told the man when he was done pouring their wine into their glasses.

"They are very efficient here." Ananda told him.

"I know. I love this place." Malcolm responded till a woman storming toward him caught his eye, "Oh no."

"I cannot believe you brought this hoe to our spot!" Merci yelled causing a scene as everyone in the quiet restaurant turned to stare.

"Can you lower you voice? You are embarrassing yourself." Malcolm spoke calmly.

"I'm not embarrassed so I will not lower my voice; you must be the one embarrassed." She continued screaming. "How dare you bring her here?"

Ananda turned a bright red getting more embarrassed by the minute. Once again, Merci had managed to ruin another evening with Malcolm. She wondered if Merci had a tracking device on Malcolm since she was always able to find him.

"Oh yeah and you can shelve your little romantic evening at the Westin. I already cancelled that reservation."

Malcolm stood up as restaurant security approached their table.

"Ma'am," They spoke addressing Merci, "You will have to lower your voice or we are going to have to ask you to leave."

"I'm not leaving unless they leave." Merci huffed.

"I apologize, we'll leave." Malcolm said as he left cash on the table and helped Ananda to her feet as they proceeded to exit the restaurant.

"I'm so sorry for this." Malcolm whispered to her.

Ananda shook her head and held her tongue until they were outside the restaurant and in the parking lot.

"You do realize how stupid you look right?" Ananda asked Merci.

"I know you're not fixin' your mouth to talk to me." Merci shouted

"I am speaking to you. You're the only one out here causing a scene and looking stupid." Ananda told her, "Didn't anyone teach you that as a lady you shouldn't shout, that you can get you point across much better if you maintain your composure."

"Compose this." Merci pushed Ananda to the ground forcing Ananda to rip her tights and scrap her knee on the concrete.

Malcolm stepped in immediately to hold Merci as Ananda jumped up off the ground. "No let her go Malcolm. I'm sick of this. She didn't get enough the first time. It's time she received a whipping so good that she won't think about laying her hands on anyone else ever."

"No, I'm not going to let you guys fight. That is enough of this foolishness." He said as he took Merci back to her car and deposited her inside.

"If you stay with this hoe tonight, don't you bring your ass home." Merci yelled, "Matter of fact, ain't nobody going nowhere." Merci jumped out the car and ran towards Ananda ramming her body into Ananda's full force causing them both to fall hard on the concrete.

Malcolm helplessly watched as the two went fist to fist and pound for pound at one another. He figured it was better to let them fight it out, so that they could hopefully move past this stage.

Ananda kept punching Merci's face and any other body part that she could reach with all her might. Merci had Ananda's short hair clutched in her fist assaulting her face with her other fist. After ten minutes of nonstop, pounding the two women began to tire. Malcolm walked up to them at this point and pulled Ananda into his arms placing her into his Range Rover. He went back and picked Merci up and placed her into her car.

"Are you happy now?" He asked her as she looked up at him exhausted with blood and tears trickling down her face.

"No." She said gasping for air. "You need to bring yourself home and stop this. I'm sick of it."

"I'm not coming to the house tonight Merci. Go home." Malcolm told her shutting her car door, making his way back to his truck.

"You okay?" Malcolm asked as soon as he entered the Range.

"I'm good." Ananda huffed out. "I'm just sick and tired of fighting all the time. Are we going to have to go through this every other time that I see you?" She asked, her face also smeared with blood. "No, I promise you." He told her.

"Good, cause I'd hate to have to kill you." Ananda told him with a smile.

Malcolm reached over and kissed Ananda careful not to put too much pressure on her swollen lip, "This feels like déjà vu." He told her with a smile.

"Yeah, but you don't have a bathtub this time to woo me."

"We're in a hundred thousand dollar truck, that's not enough to woo you?" Malcolm asked incredulously with a smile.

"I guess it will have to do since our hotel got canceled and all." Ananda joked.

Malcolm chuckled lowly as he lifted her skirt and pulled her ripped tights down her leg. "That's alright; you still have a maid at you beck and call. Your wish is my command madam."

"Oh yeah?" Ananda said with a laugh as she arched her eyebrow.

"Absolutely he said as he dipped his head in between her legs and her laughter became moans into the night.

Fourteen

"*I* can't believe that after everything we've gone through and all we've talked about you're still messing around with that girl Ananda." Merci screamed, "Are you trying to have me on death row for killing you?" Merci asked, "Because that's where we're headed if you keep playing with me."

"Stop playing stupid because I've been told you what time it was. This 'me and you' thing is not where it's at for me. I'm getting tired of this. All of this stops today."

Merci eyed him as if he were crazy. "Excuse me, what exactly is it that you will be stopping today? Enlighten me please."

"Everything, it's time I can be completely honest with you. Ananda is the woman I want to be with. This back and forth isn't fair to her when that's where I want to be anyway."

"You have some nerve you asshole." Merci continued yelling. "Some nerve indeed bringing your raggedy ass here with this nonsense. You're not even worth the fight you need to leave.

"Leave?" Malcolm questioned looking at her as if she were crazy, "this is my house why would I leave?"

"So you're saying you're willing to kick the mother of your child and daughter into the street?"

"I would never kick my daughter out. Caprice always has a place to stay."

"Oh, I see but I don't?" Merci sputtered angrily, "Well, aren't you a real piece of shit."

"I don't need this." Malcolm stated as he left her standing in the middle of the floor, grabbing his keys to the car he exited the house that he paid the mortgage on. Cranking up his truck he drove to another home and inserted a different key.

"I see you came back." Heather remarked as soon as he entered the house.

Malcolm looked at her and wished Ananda didn't live so far away. He needed her right now like he needed water to drink. He blew his mind how life worked sometimes.

"I'm only dropping by for a moment I need to kill time before I catch my flight." He lied to her he hadn't actually booked his flight yet, but was about to do so on his phone. He was making it his business to surprise Ananda today.

"Stopping through huh?" Heather snorted as she observed Malcolm standing in her front door way.

"That's all you have to say to me? You don't think you owe me an apology?"

"Yes Heather," Malcolm gave in, "I absolutely do owe you an apology for everything so please forgive me. I'm having a rough day, is it okay if I take a quick nap before I head back out?" He asked her.

Heather eyed him warily, "Of course you can take a nap, you know you don't have to ask that."

"Thanks." Malcolm told her as he headed up the stairs to the master bedroom. Taking out his cell phone he pulled up the Delta Airlines app and booked the red eye out of ATL to DCA. He needed to get to the peace and serenity that he knew only Ananda could bring.

Removing his shoes and shirt he lay on his stomach on top of the comforter in his tank top and jeans. Heather followed him into the room and straddled his back once he was comfortable. Removing the massage oil from the end table drawer she poured a little in her hand and went to work massaging the stress out his neck, back and shoulders. Malcolm welcomed her touch before he knew it he was sound asleep from Heather's therapeutic healing hands.

Waking some time later Malcolm pulled his cell phone out to get a gauge for the time and realizing that it was going upward of ten in the evening. Turning his head as his eyes readjusted to being awake and losing all traces of sleepiness he realized that Heather had lie down next to him and fallen asleep.

"Hey." Malcolm softly called out as he stood up retrieving his shirt and shoes from the chest top where Heather had placed both items. Pulling his shirt over his head he waited for her to respond when she didn't he decided to leave her be. Grabbing his keys he left her house for the airport.

****

Lying in her bed dead to the world in a deep slumber Ananda was surprised to hear her cell phone vibrating on the nightstand. Letting out a deep sigh as she rolled over to pick up her cell she opened her eyes immediately squinting from the bright light radiating from the phone.

"Hello." Her groggy voice said into the phone Malcolm's name on the screen was the only reason she answered the phone. Closing her eyes back as his deep voice massaged her eardrums like a melody from Chopin.

"I'm sorry I know your sleep, but can you come open your door?"

Ananda's brow arched in confusion, "Open my door?" She repeated slowly.

"Yes. I am at your door. Can you let me in?"

"You're here?" Ananda wondered if she were still dreaming, she seemed to be in a daze unable to get a grasp on what was happening.

Malcolm knew she was half sleep and found her disorientation adorable.

"Yes." Malcolm repeated patiently, "I'm at your front door, please let me in."

"Oh." Ananda jumped up as her brain finally registered what was going on. "I'll be right there." She told him disconnecting the call and high-tailing it to the front door to let him in.

Shifting the dead bolt back Ananda unlocked the bottom lock and opened the door to Malcolm leaning in the doorway smiling down at her.

She offered him a sheepish grin as she stepped to the side so that he could enter. "Sorry about my brain delay." Ananda tried to explain, "I wasn't expecting you."

"It's completely alright." Malcolm told her as his cell phone began to buzz and he saw Merci's name pop up on the screen. Hitting the ignore button he went ahead and cut his phone off. Tonight he didn't want any distractions he just wanted to enjoy Ananda's presence.

Now back in her bedroom Ananda sat on the bed and stared at Malcolm as he began removing his clothes. After he stripped down to nothing but his boxers he joined her on the bed. Ananda enjoyed his well-toned physique. Once he was seated comfortably she eyed him thoughtfully.

"Is everything alright? It's unlike you to show up so unexpectedly like this."

Malcolm pulled her into his arms and gave her a tight hug not wanting to let her go when she returned the gesture and held on to him harder than he was holding on to her.

"I needed to see you." He told her lying his head on top of hers not caring that she had a scarf wrapped around it. He was used to what seemed to be a standard nighttime accessory for all black women.

"Been dealing with a multitude of different things that have been depressing me lately."

"You wanna talk about it?" She asked. Ananda was aware that Malcolm led a more stressful life than anybody should have to deal with, especially when it includes someone like that psychotic Merci.

"No, I just want to hold you for tonight. Is that okay?"

"Absolutely," Ananda replied as they lay together in the bed intertwined in one another.

"Thank you for allowing me to stay." He said gently kissing her forehead.

"Anytime boo, anytime." Ananda sleepily whispered as she drifted back to sleep.

The two of them awoke the next morning to the scent of bacon cooking.

"You cooking babe?" Malcolm asked. "I didn't feel you get up."

"Because I didn't." Ananda told him as she threw back the bed covers so she could stand up.

"No, stay here." Malcolm told her as he cautiously approached the kitchen to see what was going on.

Ananda disobeying his orders followed behind him literally on his heels. Once Malcolm reached the kitchen he stopped short. "What are you doing here?" His tone was tight and aggravated.

"Because one I needed to let my husband know that Merci killed herself last night, it's all over the news in Atlanta and the two of you've been busted. I caught you." A female voice drenched in malice told him.

Ananda tried to peep around Malcolm, but he purposely held her where she was.

"Oh little miss thing didn't know, but she knows now. Malcolm is married honey."

Ananda's body went rigid as her mind was reeling from trying to process so much information at one time. Merci was dead and Malcolm was married? This was just too much for her brain to take in all at once.

"What are you talking about Heather? What happened to Merci?" Malcolm was in shock.

"If you hadn't turned your phone off, you would have known what was happening. I tried calling you several times. Good thing I found this address in my nightstand and the receipt that you sent to my email by mistake. I put two and two together and here I am to take you home so that we can deal with this Merci situation. The girls are at my mother's and the police would like the question you. According to a note they found, they say Merci committed suicide."

Picking up the first thing she saw, Ananda pushed Malcolm off her and with all her might threw the frame containing a picture of the two of them, hitting him square in the chest. Without another glance at either of them, she retreated to her room to put on her Timberland boots. She was not above a stomp out in her own place. Digging into her closet she pulled them out and put them on laced up tight. She counted to one hundred and said a prayer that she didn't kill anyone, before heading back to out to where they were. When she reached the kitchen she realized that it was empty. They had left. Only then did emotion overcome her and tears fall. She'd thought that the relationship god's had finally smiled on her and that she was going to get her happily ever after, but it looked as if the joke was on her again. She thought as she lay on the sofa and cried herself to sleep.

Fifteen

Yeah, I searched his phone, you're damn right I did. He's so stupid out here doing his thing thinking he won't get busted. So stupid! I saw the photos, the sex videos, all of it. Face deep in between her legs, her clawing the sheets, him hitting it from the back with no condom on. No respect for his marriage vows or me, nothing. But that's okay; he'll burn in hell before he claims another before me. Out here calling this woman his girlfriend, phone full of photos of her tattoos showcasing his name all over her body. He thinks he can straddle the fence and have me here being the mother to this kid; while he's out prancing around with her. I have something for them though. Yup, they'll see....he is my husband. We took vows before God and I am holding him to his word; till death do we part, even if death is the only way that I can keep him.

Sixteen

November 13, 2012

"He's married." Ananda whispered into the phone.

"Huh?" Tracey yelled into the phone slightly distracted by a rowdy group of teenagers headed her way taking up all the space in the mall. "Who's married? I can barely hear you."

"Malcolm. Malcolm is married." Ananda said in a deathly calm tone.

Tracey covered her ear as she tried to understand what Ananda was saying. The mall was overly crowded and the noise level was well above its normal octave forcing her hearing to be altered. "You and Malcolm got married? That better not be what you said because why wasn't I invited?"

"Tracey!" Ananda screamed finally getting frustrated that she had to keep repeating herself. "Listen please. No, I did not marry Malcolm! He is married to someone else! Did you hear that Tray? Malcolm is married!"

That stopped Tracey in her tracks in the middle of the mall. "Shut your mouth and call me stupid." She couldn't believe what she is hearing. "You are lying. Ana please tell me you're lying."

"It is not a game or a joke. I am not lying. Malcolm is married." Ananda's voice held finality to it.

"Wha--, how, huh?" Tracey stammered. "I don't understand any of this. Let me go outside so that I can focus. Hold on." Tracey jogged to the nearest exit in the mall and sat down on the curb once she was outside. "Ok. You have my undivided attention. Now what is going on? What makes you think that Malcolm is married?"

"I don't think Tray, I know." Ananda's voice remained calm. She didn't know how to react. She figured that her body must have been going through some kind of shock or something just as tragic because she was completely numb.

"So you're serious?" Tracey was in shock herself. She never took Malcolm as the conniving type. "How did you find out?"

"She showed up at my apartment." Ananda replied. "Have I ever told you how much I hate my life?" She attempted a small laugh.

"I don't see how you are staying so calm and able to joke about this. I'd be ready to kill someone. The fact that she showed up at your apartment and you didn't kill her says a lot."

Ananda sighed, "I don't know what to do. I haven't even spoken to him yet."

"This is crazy to me." Tracey hopped up off the curb, "Where are you? I'm coming over."

"I'm at home." Ananda said as she took off her glasses and placed them back into their case, inside of her purse.

"Okay. See you in about twenty."

"K." Ananda said as she hung up the phone and lay back in her bed that she hadn't left in over three days.

****

Back at Ananda's apartment, Tracey was doing her best to see where her friend's head was. As she sat on the loveseat across from Ananda laid out on the matching sofa, she couldn't fathom anything like this happening to her, and if it did, someone would have been cut by now, because she didn't play that and usually neither did Ananda. That's how Tracey knew for a fact that she was in her feelings.

She and Ananda had been girls for years, since they were about five years old chatting it up in kindergarten together. They had a bond that couldn't be broken and were closer than most biological sisters were. That's why Tracey's mind was reeling; she was hurt because her friend was hurt.

"I don't know what to do." Ananda whispered into the silent room.

Grateful that she had finally spoken after nearly an hour of being trapped in her own thoughts Tracey nodded her head in agreement.

"I know what you mean."

Delayed tears began cascading down Ananda's face. "I don't understand any of this. I did everything I was supposed to do. How could he do something like this to me? I am the epitome of a ride or die woman. I'm loyal, I do what he needs, and I take care of him. A random chick get outta line, I handle it. His daughter's mother acting crazy, I put her back in check. I mean what? What else did this fool need?" Ananda asked Tracey as her voice began to waver.

Tracey could barely shrug her shoulders before Ananda continued. "Right Tray? I mean, I taught this guy how to dress, how to eat properly, opened his world up to new things and he has the nerve to do something foul like this to me!" Ananda began yelling, "He's so lucky I can't get to him right now because I would try my best to make his wife a widow."

Tracey raised an amused eyebrow. Now this was the Ananda that she knew, who was beginning to resurface. She hadn't known how to take the silent, non-reacting one reeling in the middle of some pity party.

"Well you already know I got your back, whatever you want to do let's do it."

"You wouldn't even believe what this woman looks like." Ananda continued not hearing Tracey's statement. "I'm so over it. Men are dumb."

"I didn't think to ask you what she looks like." Tracey sat up on the loveseat.

"I'll show you on my laptop. You know I took to Facebook to check his page and see what the real deal is. I'm not even into social media like that. I'm a get my laptop, hold on a sec." Ananda left the room swiftly and returned almost immediately. "I go on Facebook to see if there is any truth to the comments, find the woman on his friend list." Ananda said as she logged onto

Facebook to pull up her account. "So I check her page, everything is my husband Malcolm this and my husband Malcolm that. To add insult to injury this chick was actually on my friend list!"

"You have got to be kidding me right now." Tracey's eyes widened.

"I kid you not." Ananda turned the computer to face Tracey, "This is her."

Tracey shook her head at the image staring back at her. "Oh my god, I know her!" Tracey exclaimed.

Ananda's head swung around to face Tracey's so fast that she was surprised that it didn't disconnect from her neck. Ananda's eyes narrowed as she shot daggers at Tracey's head.

"What do you mean you know her?"

Tracey's eyes were so fixated on the screen that she didn't notice Ananda staring a hole into her head.

"Around the time that I met Cameron she and I used to work the baller circuit together."

"Wait." Ananda said in disbelief waving her hand across the front of her face, "You and this girl Heather used to strip together?"

"Among other things." Tracey whispered.

"This is craziness."

Tracey shook her head, "I'm so sorry Ana. I had no idea that she had even gotten married. I lost touch with her once I began dating Cameron. I tried my best to put that whole other life behind me."

Ananda wanted to do physical damage to something. Anything. She didn't see how her day could get any worse. She jumped off the sofa when she felt tears threaten and ran to her bathroom shutting the door behind her. Standing in front of the mirror taking in her appearance she was really a sore sight to see. Her eyes were bloodshot, her normally short curly hair was lying flat on her head and she had a migraine the size of Mount Everest that was pounding intensely.

Tracey rose off the loveseat and knocked on the bathroom door. "Ana, you alright in there? Why not call up Malcolm and see what the real deal is. You haven't even spoken to him since all of this went down right. Why not wait and see what he has to say."

"What can he say Tray." Ananda said as she reluctantly opened the bathroom door to face her friend. "What explanation can someone possibly give for marrying someone else? Please tell me. I need someone to explain that to me. He's been blowing my phone up non-stop, but I don't know what to say to him right now."

Tracey pulled Ananda into a hug. "I don't really know, but what I do know is I wouldn't trip off her anyway. She looks like a horse to me, so you know he didn't marry her for her looks."

That comment made Ananda burst into laughter, "Why are you so stupid?" She said pulling out of Tracey's embrace, rolling her eyes. "Thanks for trying to make me feel better, with your crazy self."

Tracey laughed. "I'm just saying if you need one plus in this situation at least you have that one."

"Yeah, I guess."

"Are you going to speak to him?"

"No, I'm biding my time. Have to make sure that I have everything lined up and in order." Ananda said as she hit print on her laptop. "I do believe I am going to invite Mister Malcolm to dinner tonight."

"Do you think that is a good idea?" Tracey asked a little apprehensive. She knew how Ananda's temperament could be and didn't want her getting into any kinds of trouble. "Don't go getting arrested dealing with this fool."

"Trust me. I'm cool. It'll be fine." Ananda reassured her with a devious smile. "You still know how to get into contact with Heather?"

Tracey had a feeling of dread, "I'm sure I could if I needed too, but why would you want to contact her?"

Ananda winked at her and said "Who said that I wanted to contact her. It's just good to know that you can if the need ever arose to do so.

Tracey knew all too well what that meant and it was in her best interest to be ready in the event everything hit the fan and in situations like this one, they usually did.

Seventeen

$\mathcal{A}$nanda watched as Malcolm approached her. He had flown in last minute to meet up with her. Standing up to receive his embrace she wanted to melt in his arms like she used too, but knew that she couldn't and probably never would again. She knew that Malcolm was a liar; she finally had proof and wanted to see what he had to say about the situation.

"I love you." Malcolm whispered into Ananda's hair as he hugged her. "We can fix this."

"Mmmhmmn, I bet you do." Ananda replied with a slight attitude as she broke away from his hug and took a seat across from him at the table. "And I am more than positive that we cannot."

Staring at her from across the table at the historic Old Ebbitt's Grill in D.C., he knew that it was going to be an uphill battle getting Ananda to understand. She was already in a funky mood.

Taking in her honey dipped skin encased in a black chic jumpsuit, five inch strappy black stiletto's clutching her French pedicured toes; her silky curly hair pulled back into a Mohawk, gold hoops hanging from her delicate ears and big dark brown eyes that were currently narrowed silently throwing daggers at him; Malcolm knew it was going to be a long dinner. Shaking his head, he sighed. He wasn't in the mood to have an argument with Ananda today. He was dealing with a lot as it was.

"What's wrong with you?" He asked eyeing her intently trying to see where the conversation would lead.

"A lot, actually." Ananda spoke with venom etched in her voice. "You have some nerve sitting over there like everything is okay."

"Everything is okay to me" Malcolm told her, "You the one that came in with an attitude."

"You know what I'm talking about!" Ananda exclaimed in a loud whisper.

Malcolm stared into her angry eyes for a moment then leaned back in his chair remaining calm, refusing to let her get a rise out of him. "Actually I don't, enlighten me. What are you talking about?"

Ananda leaned in close, "I'm talking about a strange woman showing up at my apartment. I'm talking about this." She said as she dug into her wallet, pulled out a folded piece of paper, and handed it to him.

Malcolm didn't know what was on the paper, but he knew whatever it was had to be serious enough for her to print out off the computer and bring to him in person. Unfolding the paper he closed his eyes momentarily once he saw what was on printed on it trying to think fast, wishing he could turn back the hands of time and change everything.

"Well?" Ananda asked interrupting Malcolm's thoughts. Malcolm kept his eyes closed.

Ananda took her foot encased in her five inch heels and kicked Malcolm as hard as she could in his shin. She didn't agree to see and have lunch with him for him to think that he was going to ignore her.

"Yo!" Malcolm's eyes snapped open as he grabbed his shin. He had to check himself because he wanted to snatch her up by the throat. "What you doing? Calm down."

"Keep playing with me and I'll show you anything but calm." Ananda warned. She knew that Malcolm was trying to stall and she wasn't going to give him the satisfaction.

"So all of it is true?" She asked pointing at the paper. "You are married?"

"You can't believe everything you see on the computer. You know people can make anything real online." Malcolm said smoothly avoiding answering the question.

Unable to contain her anger Ananda smacked Malcolm hard across his face. "That's not an answer. And no I'm not believing everything I see online. You act as if this woman wasn't in my home." Ananda was getting more and more angry as the conversation went on. Malcolm was taking her for a joke and she was about to go off. She could feel it. "You tell me right now if it's true or not." She snapped at him, "I'm not up in here to play with you. This is serious, now answer the question." She was ready to jump across the table and strangle him half to death.

A stunned Malcolm was reeling from being smacked as he attempted to reach for her hand Ananda swiftly moved her hands off the table and placed them on her lap. Malcolm put his hands back on his side of the table and broke eye contact with Ananda. Ananda began blinking rapidly.

"It's true isn't it?" She whispered, trying to forbid the tears that wanted to fall from falling. Malcolm's withdrawn demeanor told her everything she needed to know.

"It's not what you think." He finally said bringing his eyes to meet hers again.

Ananda shut her eyes finding it hard to swallow. It seemed like the air around her was smothering her forcing her not to be able to breathe.

"Baby, listen to me." Malcolm stared at Ananda trying to get through to her. He loved this woman with all his heart and he needed her to understand that the decision he made hadn't been based on love. He had done it out of necessity.

Ananda had so many emotions raging through her body that she was afraid to move because she knew if she moved even an inch she was going to be across the table attacking Malcolm and then locked up for attempted murder, so she stayed in her chair shaking rapidly praying for strength through this.

"How could you do something like this to me? I thought we were a family and you had a whole other family this whole time. So what was I, someone for you to play with? I thought I was in a serious relationship and you were playing games?" Ananda sniffed. She was hurt and she needed some type of explanation from him, something to help her understand why.

"Everything isn't always what it seems." Malcolm began trying to explain. He hated seeing Ananda like this. She was usually the strong one all the time, crying wasn't part of her MO. To know that he had reduced her to this was killing him.

"And what? I wasn't good enough?" Ananda accused him.

Malcolm took a deep sigh. "It's not that."

"Ok, so what is it then? Huh!" Ananda wasn't with all this beating around the bush nonsense. "Just tell me like it is. Get to the point."

"She's always been there for me whenever I needed anything, she's always been there. It's weird, but I've loved her from the moment that I lay eyes on her." He paused, "And then I met you not too long after. I never planned on you. You made me feel what I felt when I first met her times ten."

"What!" Ananda shook her head. "That is irrelevant! Once you get married none of that stuff matters. You have some nerve. You know what, I don't need this, and I don't need you." Standing up swiftly Ananda didn't give a damn about how foolish she looked in the restaurant. She wanted out now.

Malcolm quickly reached out and grabbed Ananda's arm. He let her go almost as fast as he grabbed her when he noticed people around them were beginning to stare.

"Baby, please don't cause a scene. Just hear me out for a minute." Malcolm pleaded with her. He knew Ananda wasn't about this life and took her relationship with him very seriously. He also knew that he had less than two seconds to explain something that she could understand before he lost her forever. "Please." He begged offering up pleading eyes to hers.

Ananda stared down at him long and hard taking in his sad brown eyes. *My Malcolm* she thought. The man I wanted to spend the rest of my life with. Tears filled her eyes and threatened to spill as he continued looking at him taking in his appearance. There he sat with his curly hair that she loved to run her fingers through, his dark brown skin freshly lotioned up and glistening. She could tell that he had been hitting the gym hard the way his arms were bulging out of his rolled up sleeves. He looked good, Ananda hated to admit, but none of that excused his actions. None of it.

"Sit back down please. At least let me explain." Malcolm continued to beg her.

Ananda had never seen Malcolm beg in his life, this was a new development. Sighing in defeat, she sat back down and figured that she owed it to herself to hear what he had to say.

Malcolm knew Ananda well enough to know she had an attitude and once she was in that state, it was hard to get her out of it.

"Ok, I'm listening." Ananda stared at him like he had two heads. She didn't know the man sitting in front of her. This wasn't her best friend, her boo, the man she had thought he was.

"Baby," Malcolm began taking her hand into his, ecstatic with the small victory of her letting him hold her hand. "Just bear with me through this. I need you more than ever now."

Ananda stared at him waiting for him to continue. "I love you, you are my world. I never should have gotten involved with you, but my heart wouldn't let me not get to know you." Ananda blinked but remained unmoved by what he said. Malcolm began to panic, Ananda wasn't the silent type. She had something to say about everything, so the fact that she wasn't saying anything carried a lot of weight for Malcolm.

"You know things with me and Merci weren't going great. We were having so many problems because she was fighting her own demons, not coping well with our breakup and me finally leaving her. Then for her to commit suicide, life is crazy."

This wasn't news to Ananda; she had known that Merci was the sneaky, conniving type because they had their own back-story of drama. Merci was a loose cannon. She and Ananda had fought on numerous occasions because Merci didn't know what to say out of her mouth or how to respect boundaries and Ananda was having none of it. Merci dying didn't move her either way, she was happy that she was gone.

"So this all has to do with you being selfish?" Malcolm silently rejoiced when Ananda asked him that question. A speaking Ananda was better than a quiet one any day.

"Something like that."

"I'm confused, what does this have to do with you being married and still feeling like it was okay to date me?" Ananda felt like they were going off topic. Malcolm was trying to draw her into his story without dealing with what he had done.

"Everything."

Ananda laughed in disbelief at his audacity. "Ohhhh, so that's it?" Ananda shook her head from side to side. "You are a piece of work you hear me. That's the only answer that you're going to give me. I may not have the biggest house on the block, or a ton of money in my bank account, but all my bills are paid, I drive my own car and I am about to move into my own house and you sit there and pretty much say that the reason you didn't tell me you were married is because you saw me and just had to know me?" The hurt in Ananda's voice was so apparent.

"I feel so betrayed by you. You were supposed to be my best friend. I thought that we could talk about anything. You were supposed to protect me from stuff like this. I told you all about the men in my past and the things I had gone through and you are just like every other man in my life. You're actually much worse; none of them has ever done anything like this to me. You were living a double life, like who does that? You're a liar and a phony and I'm sorry that I ever met you." Ananda snapped at him as the forbidden tears slid down her face, mad that this man was able to affect her like this.

"Baby, please don't cry. All I'm asking you to do is give me time to fix all of this. Please."

"Fix what? You are married! There is no fixing that." Ananda stood up again, "And I won't be a part of it. I wish you the best. And when you go to sleep tonight, you thank God that I've been working on my temper and the new me doesn't have time for this, because if I was who I used to be who knows what would happen." Malcolm gazed up at her and knew that she was serious; he's pretty sure the old Ananda would have had him meet her at dawn for a show down in the street.

"Baby, I'm just asking you to understand."

"There is nothing to understand. End of discussion. I hope that you enjoy the rest of your day. As for me, I've had enough."

Ananda turned her back on Malcolm and proceeded to walk toward the exit of the restaurant. She was done with this foolishness; walking down the sidewalk to her car she was glad when she reached it. Sliding into the driver's seat she promptly put her head down on the steering wheel and proceeded to cry for the life she'd once wanted but knew that she would never have.

Eighteen

"This is a pleasant surprise" Hunter was shocked when Lorna

patched through a call from Ananda to him.

"Hello Mr. Lewis." Ananda began, "I was wondering if you had any new job opportunities coming up. I need a change of scenery and would love an assignment somewhere away from the DMV area.

"Ananda, please call me Hunter." He requested of her again.

"I apologize, Hunter."

"Thank you, no apology needed." He smiled considering it a small victory that she'd finally called him Hunter. "I do have some local ads that need casting and you do fit the look. Can you come to New York for the next week or so?" Or forever he thought to himself.

"Absolutely, I have nothing whatsoever going on to keep me here."

"Good I'll have Lorna book your flight and I'll see you in a couple of hours."

"Thank you so much." Ananda exclaimed glad to have something to occupy her time with for a while. "I'll head to the airport in about an hour."

"Alright, I'll see you soon." Hunter said as they disconnected the call.

Several hours later Hunter glanced up from the notes on his desk when he received a knock at his door. "Come in." He called out.

Ananda strutted into his office as if she owned the world. No one would ever be able to tell the inner turmoil that she was experiencing that had her heart broken into a million pieces. She was surprised that it still allowed her to live. She was almost certain that a heart as broken as hers should have stopped working and that she should be six feet under by now.

Hunter stood when he saw Ananda come through his office door.

"How does it feel being Colgate's million dollar woman?" He asked as he held out his hands for her to shake.

Ananda gave him a soft grateful smile. "It's still very surreal." She told him with a smile. I still can't believe that I am so fortunate to have such a blessing like this come my way. It's amazing."

"I'm indebted to your manager forever. Without him we would have never found you and you us. Does he know that you're here now seeking new work? I haven't heard from him in a while."

To Ananda's horror tears began to slide down her face at the mention of Malcolm's name.

Hunter was taken back when he saw the moisture on her face. "Was it something I said?" He asked her as he went behind his desk and produced a box of tissue and offered it to her.

Ananda shook her head as she relieved him of the box of tissue taking one out to pat her eyes. She was now angry for allowing herself to show emotional weakness especially in front of someone like Hunter Lewis.

Hunter took in her defeated look and came back around to the front of his desk, so that he could console her. Even though he wasn't the type to get personally involved, there was something about Ananda that had intrigued him from the first moment that he had laid eyes on her. Gently putting his arms around her he enveloped her into a hug and placed her head on his shoulder.

"It's okay. I apologize for whatever I said that triggered this reaction from you. I know that you're a strong woman Ananda, but if you want to talk to me about whatever is bothering you I'm willing to offer a listening ear." He was genuinely concerned. He knew that whatever the problem it was serious enough to allow him to touch her. He wasn't oblivious as to how she felt about him. He sensed her desire to keep him at a distance and that he rubbed her the wrong way. However, he was happy for the opportunity to show her a different side of him.

"I'm so sorry, I'm usually not so emotional but the last few weeks have really been taking a toll on me."

Hunter guided her to one of the chairs in front of his desk and sat next to her. He gently patted her back, not saying anything, waiting for her to continue when she was ready.

"I just found out that Malcolm is married." She began. "He was my boyfriend and I loved him. I was looking forward to marrying him one day, having his babies and carrying his last name. None of that will happen now.

Hunter remained quiet. He hoped that she would gain some comfort through his silence.

"I know that I must seem pathetic to you." Ananda sniffled as she lifted her head off of his shoulder, "I didn't mean to breakdown. All of this happened so suddenly, my feelings are still a little raw."

"It's alright." Hunter said as he sat back in his chair giving her a moment to compose herself.

"May I offer you a drink?" Hunter stood up and headed toward the mini bar at the far side of his office.

"No thank you."

"You'll have one." Hunter told her as he fixed them both a vodka and orange juice mix and handed one glass to her.

Ananda removed it from his hands gratefully and finished it in one gulp handing the glass back to a surprised Hunter.

"You do know that there was alcohol in there right? You shouldn't suck it down quite that fast."

"I know. May I have another one please?"

Hunter took her empty glass and handed her his as he made another drink for himself. When he finished making her drink he noticed that she had finished her second one as well and sat the empty glass on his desk before he had a chance to sit back down in his chair.

"I'm not trying to sound like your dad or anything, but you may want to take it easy on the drinks a little." Hunter said to her as he sipped slowly on his drink.

"I usually don't drink like this. I just have a lot going on and alcohol makes me feel better. It allows me the opportunity to forget for a few hours." Ananda looked at him coyly and for the first time really took him in. Hunter Lewis was an extremely attractive man and it's not that Ananda hadn't noticed before it was just that she was dating Malcolm. Furthermore, Hunter's pompous personality generally turned her off, but somehow tonight he seemed different. He was being more attentive and didn't appear to have an agenda other than a real concern for her feelings. She couldn't tell whether he was tolerable after all or if it either her loneliness or the alcohol was clouding her judgment. Whatever it is she was starting to get turned on and wanted Hunter right this second.

"You okay?" Hunter asked her noticing that she had been staring at him for several minutes and not saying anything.

Ananda stood and came to stand in front of Hunter "Not really, but I will be soon." Removing his glass of vodka and orange juice from his hand and placing it on his desk she leaned down and kissed him.

Hunter broke off the kiss almost immediately. He knew Ananda didn't know how attracted he was to her because if she did she wouldn't be playing this game with him. "I don't think that's a good idea." He attempted to rise from his chair, but Ananda was too quick for him and sat on his lap forcing him to sink back into the chair.

"Who said anything about having ideas, good or bad?" She said breathlessly as she leaned in for another kiss, this time wrapping her arm around his neck so he couldn't jerk away from her. Hunter tried to fight the feeling at first but as Ananda deepened the kiss he knew there was no way he could resist her.

"You sure this is something you want to do?" He asked breaking the kiss momentarily. "I don't want to take advantage of what you're going through at the moment."

"Shhh, I want this. I need it." Ananda told him as he recaptured her lips into a sensual kiss that she felt radiating through her entire body.

"I promise you won't regret it." Hunter told her as he rose from the chair with her in his arms and lowered her to the floor of his office. For the better part of the evening their lovemaking sounds echoed through his office.

"Mr. Lewis, your seven o'clock is here waiting in the lobby." Lorna knocked once before opening the door to Hunter's office stopping short, eyes widening as she found him and Ananda asleep on the floor in each other's arms. Shocked and in tears she silently closed the door and fled from the office not understanding how he could do something like that to her. Ananda works for him, much like any other employee and he doesn't seem to have any problem having relations with her. Gathering her things from her desk she left the office for the rest of the evening. She would let Mr. Lewis figure out what to tell his clients himself. She didn't care what happened at this particular moment. All she knew was that she was going home and that was the end of it for right now. Any issues he had with her leaving early would have to be dealt with another day.

Nineteen

"Stop calling me." Ananda screamed into the phone before she hung up.

Ananda's cell phone instantly began to ring again and she was annoyed. Malcolm was attempting to contact her for the umpteenth time and she had nothing whatsoever to say to him. The last month had been hell on earth for her and she was having a hard time coping as it was.

"Yes!" Ananda spoke with an attitude when the phone rang again and Malcolm's name popped onto the screen of her cell. "Why do you keep calling me back to back like this?"

"Because I want you to talk to me."

"I'm done talking. There is nothing left to say. Why won't you leave me alone?"

"Because I love you."

Ananda gave an exasperated sigh, "Malcolm," she began as patiently as she could muster, "what do you want from me? You have a wife, why not go and live your life? I am unclear as to why we are even having a conversation."

"Ananda, I want you. Everything isn't what it seems." Malcolm paused, searching for the right words. "I don't love her the way that I love you."

"I'm not really sure what to tell you. All I know is that I am all cried out. I'm done with the drama and the tears, I'm just done. Even if you won't respect your marriage I will. And just so you fully understand what's happening here, I -- meaning me -- Ananda is moving on. I want to date and have fun and I going to do it, excuse me -- I am doing it."

"Damn, how you trying to date someone else already?" Malcolm shouts angrily, "It's only been four weeks. Hoes have more loyalty than you."

"Whoa, pump your breaks and watch your mouth. The only hoe here is you. I've had your daughter's mother pop up at my place as well as your wife. If anyone is the hoe in this situation it is clear to see that you win that category hands down." Ananda continued calmly, "Talking about loyalty, you need not speak about something you have no idea about. The only person that you are loyal to is yourself. Your self-righteous ass sitting over there judging me, you have obviously lost your mind." She began to yell into the phone with all sense of calm gone from her voice. She is now upset with herself that she had allowed him to get her riled up like this.

"I am free and single and have no need or desire to be tied up with someone who is neither. I'm done with you. Have a nice life and please stop harassing me." She told him hanging up the phone visibly upset. She couldn't lie and say that she didn't miss Malcolm because she did.That's why she continued taking his calls when she knew that she shouldn't. The more she took the calls the more he was starting to break down her defenses and get to her and she knew she couldn't have that. So she chose to get smart and pick a fight instead so that he wouldn't suspect that she was weakening. Even in her weakened state however, her pride refused to allow her to be his or anyone's mistress.

Needing to get her mind off Malcolm and get a quick pick me up Ananda dialed Tracey's number. The phone rang five times before Tracey's voicemail picked up and her bubbly voice came across the line, "You've reached Tray, please leave a message."

"Tray, this is Ana. Give me a call when you get a chance I need to talk." Ananda was disappointed. Tracey had been MIA lately ever since she and Cameron had seemed to work out their differences. Cam appeared to finally understand that Tracey was crazy and wasn't going to have him stepping out on her without a fight or confrontation every single time and sooner or later the media buzz would get him traded before he could blink. Also, with Tracey deciding to hit the road with him full-time while he was in season she rarely got to see her friend anymore.

This sucks Ananda thought to herself, scrolling through her contacts list until she saw Hunter's name. Deciding to make his day she dialed his office number. They had enjoyed a fun filled week the last time she in New York doing nothing more than but working hard and making love. He had been just what the doctor had ordered. By the time she got back home she was much more relaxed and her bank account enriched. All in all she would have to say that it was a successful trip. The only little quirk in their week-long rendezvous was Hunter's assistant, Lorna.

She knew the young woman had a thing for Hunter and definitely didn't care for Ananda from day one, but that was of no consequence to Ananda. Hunter had told her that on that first night his assistant had walked in and found them on the floor in his office. She spoken to him about it and he said she seemed to be okay, but Ananda knew better. She was a woman and the only reason the assistant had brought it to his attention is because she wanted him to reveal how he felt about it.

"Hunter Lewis' office how may I help you?" Lorna answered on the first ring.

Ananda rolled her eyes knowing that Lorna had seen her number on the caller ID and was playing dumb. "Hello Lorna, it's Ananda, is Hunter available?"

"For you? No." Lorna answered snidely.

Ananda chuckled lowly, "Is that right?" She spoke to her slowly, patiently as if to a child behaving poorly, "Lorna, I know Hunter would be very angry with you if he knew that I called and you didn't let him know that I was on the phone. Can you please be a dear and buzz him for me. There is no room in my schedule for childish games today."

Lorna huffed hard into the phone "Hold on." She said with plenty of attitude placing the phone on hold.

After listening for nearly five minutes to the classical music that played while her call was on hold; Ananda wondered if Lorna really hadn't let Hunter know that she was on the phone or if she was trying to test her patience by leaving her on hold indefinitely.

"Hunter here." His voice materialized on the other end of the phone before she could complete the thought.

"Hi. It's Ananda."

"Hello." He drawled out in his New York accent, his tone instantly softening.

I knew that little heifer wouldn't let him know who was on the other end of the phone. Ananda thought.

"To what do I owe the pleasure of your time?"

Ananda smiled, Hunter was such a cornball, but she loved it. "I was just lonely and called you. I didn't want anything."

"You miss me don't you?" He said with a hint of a smile in his voice.

"How'd you guess?" Ananda promptly responded as she shook her head smiling "What are you up too?"

Hunter leaned back in his chair and put his feet on his desk loosening his tie. "Wrapping up a long day at the office and looking for a distraction, any ideas on who could help me?"

Ananda giggled, "Of course I do. Are you glued to the office for the rest of the day or would you mind coming to Maryland and having dinner with me."

"I own the company. I'm never glued to the office." He told her. "How about I have Lorna make us dinner reservations at SAX in DC and we'll enjoy each other's company and take in a burlesque show. How does that sound to you?"

"That sounds perfect. I've wanted to see what SAX was like after reading so many great reviews about it." Ananda was more than amused knowing how Lorna was going to feel about having to make their dinner and show reservations.

"Alright, sounds like a plan. I'll pick you up around seven tonight."

"Yay. I'm so excited." Ananda was glowing as she hung up the phone so that she could begin to go through her closet and find something to wear for the evening.

No sooner had she hung up with Hunter did her cell phone begin to vibrate in her hand. Seeing Tracey's name flash across the screen she answered on the first ring.

"Bout time you call somebody back. Where have you been?" Ananda lightly scolded her.

"Girl, I'm sorry. Who knew that following Cameron from city to city would be such an exhausting fulltime job?"

Ananda laughed, "You should have known that. I don't see how you do it."

"If you're married to a pro athlete I don't see how you have a choice. That's one thing I have learned from Jackie Christie, remember how we used to talk about how crazy she was back in the day following her husband everywhere? Now that I'm living this life, I completely understand. Wherever Cameron is I am. I am not having it."

"You don't have to justify anything to me, I completely understand. I'm just asking you not to forget about your friend in the process."

"Ana, you know that I would never forget about my home girl. What has been going on? I know I haven't really been around after the whole Malcolm fiasco. How is that going?"

"It's not. I don't know actually. I think I'm starting to feel sorry for him."

"Wait, what? Why feel sorry for him! He's the one who was messing around on you, his baby mamma and a wife."

"I know, but he says he doesn't really love her and that he really wants to be with me."

"Ananda, do you hear yourself. You have got to come up out of this. Malcolm is a liar and a manipulator. Do not and I repeat do not fall into his mess. Please."

Ananda heard what Tracey was saying and it all made sense, but she wasn't sure what to do. She couldn't make her heart stop feeling what it was feeling and she was still in love with Malcolm.

"I went out with Hunter." Ananda told her changing the subject.

"Don't think you getting off the hook that easy about Malcolm. I'm not letting you off the hook that easily, but since you're trying to change the subject I'll play along for right now. How is Hunter?" Tracey asked.

"He's good. He's coming down from the city today to have dinner with me."

"Nice. So if you're going out with him, why do you insist on staying hung up on Malcolm? "

"Because you can't help who you love Tracey."

"You most certainly can. Love is a choice. You choose and Malcolm chose someone else and you need to do the same. This is why I told you I worry about you when you first met him remember. You seem to pick the worst guys for yourself."

"I find it amazing that you sit on your high horse over there and you're the same one just talking about having to stay fused to her husband's hip while he's on the road so he won't cheat on you.

Aren't you the very same woman who dragged me into DC to kick in his mistress' door?"

"See, you trying to hit below the belt now." Tracey is catching an attitude now, "The difference between you and I is that Cameron is my husband. I have every right to fight to keep my marriage together. Malcolm is married to someone else who will be fighting to keep her marriage intact too. Men never leave their wives for the side piece Ananda. Don't you know that?" Tracey changed her tone to one of sadness. "I feel sorry for you. There is nothing you will be able to do to make this man leave his wife for you and even if he did, would you really want him?"

"Well what would you suggest Mrs. Mouth Almighty?" Now it is Ananda who has an attitude of her own.

"Go out with Hunter, he is free and available -- that you know of anyway. Why not have·fun with him and see what happens? Even if it doesn't go anywhere, at least it will help you get over Malcolm.

"That's easier said than done." Ananda grumbled.

"Well not that it's that big a deal, but since you're so stuck on Malcolm, you may want to know that I did track down Heather and had a pleasant chat with her."

Ananda's blood instantly went from heated to boiling. "What do you mean you had a pleasant chat with her? You're not supposed to be engaging with the enemy."

"To be honest she's not the enemy, you are."

"Okay what a minute. Whose side are you on?"

"I'm always on your side Ana, except in this situation because you're dead wrong and you know it."

"How am I wrong? I didn't know Malcolm was married and I haven't been with him since, so how am I wrong?"

"Because you're thinking about going back and that's because you don't know Heather and you don't care how she feels, but her feelings are hurt and she really loves him. Did you ever stop to think about if you were in her shoes?"

"I know how to keep a man, so I wouldn't be in her shoes."

"You know how to keep a man huh?" Tracey paused, "That's your answer? Don't you think if that were true you'd be married by now?"

Ananda hung up on Tracey. She didn't need her so called friend on the other end of the phone line judging her, as if she has room to judge anyone. Tracey seemed to forget that before she met Cameron she was just a high priced call girl who for the right amount of money would do just about anything sexually. Cameron came along and liked her so much he cleaned her up and took her off the street and out of that life by marrying her. Now Tracey had the nerve to look down on Ananda like her shit didn't stink.

The phone rang a few minutes later with Tracey on the other end.

"What." Ananda snapped into the phone.

"I'm sorry. I should have never said that. I took things way too far and I apologize. I love you and I just want you to make better decisions to take care of you."

"I love you too and I appreciate the apology. Can we agree to disagree and leave this topic alone for right now? I want to get ready for my date and have a nice evening without this being on my mind."

"My lips are sealed."

"Thanks Tray. I'll talk to you later." Ananda hung up the phone and walked into her closet to see what she could wear that would make Hunter want to stay the rest of the week.

Twenty

$\mathcal{M}$alcolm had made it his business to be on his best behavior around Heather since the showdown at Ananda's apartment. He felt as if he were walking on eggshells and was uncomfortable in his own skin.

"Are you hungry?" Heather asked Malcolm. "Caprice, Tatiana and I have eaten already."

"No, I'm okay." Malcolm no longer trusted Heather's cooking. She tried make it seem like things between them were back on track and normal, but he knew better and wasn't falling for this charade that she was putting on. She'd been acting funny ever since he'd seen the police pictures of Merci's body hanging in their kitchen and a copy of the suicide note. He didn't buy this suicide nonsense for a minute. There was too much blood and Merci wasn't the type to try and kill herself when she was all about taking things head on. Killing herself would have been like giving in and giving up and that just wasn't her style.

"Want to talk about it?" Heather asked him, "Seems like you have a lot on your mind."

"Did you kill Merci?" Malcolm asked her point blank. He was tired of the games. He needed to be able to sleep at night. This one eye open thing wasn't working for him.

Heather was genuinely appalled. "What would make you think that way and ask me something like that? I'm offended."

Malcolm was unmoved, "You didn't answer the question."

"Merci was suffering from her own demons per your own words. She didn't need me to kill her. She killed herself long ago. I guess trying to accept everything was too much for her. But either way she was going to accept what was. She did us all a favor if you ask me."

"I am asking you and I would appreciate a direct answer."

Heather focused her eyes on Malcolm, "No, I did not kill Merci. Did I want her to get it together and leave you alone? Yes. Did I wish she would disappear? Hell, yes. Am I sad that she is gone? No. Good riddance to her, but I swear to you, I did not kill her."

"Okay." Malcolm said after studying her for a minute. "Is it okay if you keep Caprice and Tatiana? I have to make a trip. I should be back early in the morning."

"Of course I'll keep them. Caprice is my baby and we're going to have a great time while you're gone."

"Cool. I'll touch base with you when I touch down." Malcolm went to their bedroom to toss some clothes in a bag and head out.

Apprehensive, Malcolm stood outside the door for a long time before finally building his courage up and knocking on the door.

A knock at the front door halted Ananda's pen. It was now three in the morning and she had no idea who would be coming to see her at this late hour. Putting the journal that she had been writing back under her bed she walked to the door and looked through the peephole. Shocked she opened the door to stare at the person responsible for her hurt.

"What are you doing here?" She eventually managed to choke out.

"I had to see you and I knew you would never agree to see me, so I took the red eye here to get to you and make you understand."

Ananda was at a loss for words. The last time that Malcolm had been at her place was when Heather had shown up unexpectedly like an extra from Set It Off.

"Are you alone? No surprise pop ups this time right?"

"I'm alone. And I really need to speak with you. May I come in?"

Ananda debated about whether that was a good idea or not, figuring that it wasn't she still stepped back and allowed him to enter. Closing the door once he passed her. Sitting on the couch she looked up at him as he remained standing.

"What do you have to say that you couldn't say over the phone?"

"I don't know what to say." He knelt down in front of her. "I just knew that I had to get here to see you so that you could talk, face to face."

"Malcolm I feel like we're going around in circles. Talking about the same thing and it all ends with the same result. You are married. You were married when I met you. Why you started a relationship with me in the first place is something I still can't comprehend. I never would have suspected that you would be capable of all of this, but you are the reason for all this madness in so many lives. And worst of all, you brought all of this drama into my life."

"I know and I apologize. I've just needed to talk to someone ever since I found out that Merci killed herself." Ananda head snapped back, "Are you serious?" Her voice barely containing her contempt, "But why me, why not your wifey?" I'm here to see you because I just need to talk to somebody that I can trust. I know that you hate me right now but I don't know where else to turn. You know that the police have declared Merci's death a suicide?" "Yes," Ananda said shaking her head. "I can't believe it though, that woman was relentless about what she wanted. I just don't see it."

"You and me both. I still don't believe she killed herself, but the Merci I knew wasn't built with that kind of weakness in her. She never would have left Caprice and Tatiana. No matter how crazy things were, she never would have left them." Malcolm felt the moisture on his face and turned away from Ananda so she wouldn't see.

Ananda was so shocked to see that Malcolm felt vulnerable enough to cry in front of her, her heart just melted. Sliding down to sit on the floor next to him she pulled his head into her lap and began to stroke his hair.

"Don't cry Malcolm. I'm so sorry. I had no idea. I mean Merci was crazy and all, but I didn't want anything as extreme as death to happen to her." Ananda told him, though in actuality it didn't bother her in the least that Merci was gone.

"Yeah, it's been so crazy at home."

"I'll bet it has been. How is Heather?" Ananda asked, unable to find a way to keep that woman's name from coming up.

"I'm not sure. She's acting like everything is okay, but the house feels more like being on a minefield and waiting for a time bomb to go off – and she's ticking."

"I imagine that she is."

"I'm getting a divorce." Ananda stopped stroking his hair in mid motion as her heart slammed into her chest. "What?" She whispered. "Are you being for real right now or is this a joke?"

"I'm being for real. I filed separation papers with my lawyer before I made the trip up here." Ananda tilted her head to the side as Malcolm sat up. "I need to be with you and I know that you will never be with me as long as I'm married, so I'm getting a divorce. You have to be in my life. Please tell me you'll be in my life."

Ananda stared into his chestnut brown eyes for a longtime before nodding her head and allowing the words to pass through her lips. "Yes, I'll be a part of your life, no matter what."

"No matter what." He said again and again as he gently kissed her lips while guiding her to the floor to explore the body he thought he'd never get to explore again.

Twenty-One

*S*itting *in the middle of the new hardwood floor she'd recently*

had installed with her legs folded beneath her body, the separation papers encircling her. The smoke billowing out around her as she dragged another long puff off her Newport cigarette into her air deprived lungs she sat in the foyer eyes glued to the front door willing her husband to come home. Encased in darkness with the children fast asleep, the reddish spark from her slender white nicotine addiction the only thing illuminating the eerily still house as the clock struck three a.m. Her ears were being serenaded by the sound of Etta James singing All I Could Do Was Cry from the iPad he'd bought her as a birthday present the previous year. She listened as the words of the song etched themselves into her soul All I could do, all I could do was cry, All I could do was cry, I was losing the man that I loved, and all I could do was cry.

The whore doesn't see me as a threat she thought, oh but she will. She will learn that to underestimate me is to sign a death wish. I hope that she has made things right with her maker because the whore her husband repeatedly sexed shall be seeing her maker real soon, very soon. I, his wife will personally see to it.

A year ago her tears would have made a steady rhythmic descent down her face, but not now. Now, at this moment in time she has decided that she has dealt with more than her fair share of heartache and now she would make sure that he will deal with the consequences of his actions! She knew that most people believed in letting karma handle their problems for them, but her time and her patience was short and karma will take far too long. She was going to see to it that everything happens as it should even if it was the last thing that she was to do on this earth. She would make him see without a doubt that she would always be his one and only, "till death do us part." Separation papers be damned....

Twenty-Two

$\mathcal{E}$ntering Hunter's office, Amanda had jumped an unplanned flight to New York to sign a new contract for a deal he had landed for her.

"Lorna, I'm here to see Hunter, I'm just going to drop right in." She told the young woman as she sashayed past her without waiting for her response.

"You can't just go in there." Lorna exclaimed jumping up to head her off.

Too late. Ananda thought as she entered Hunter's office and shut the door in Lorna's face locking it.

Hunter glanced up from the tense phone conversation and smiled instantly when he saw Ananda standing by the door all smiles. "I have to go." Hunter spoke into the receiver disconnecting the call.

"You love surprising me."

"Well I figured since you had papers for me to sign and I haven't seen you in about a week I would just come on up and say hello."

Hunter walked up to her and embraced her in a hug, "I could have just faxed you the papers you know." He said releasing her.

"I do know, but then you never would have gotten the chance to see me and why would you pass up on an opportunity such as this." She threw her hands above her head in a dramatic fashion so that he could take in all of her.

"Well, I can't argue with you there. You seem like you're in an amazing mood today." Hunter told her as he went back to his desk to retrieve the papers that he needed her to sign. "I am, got some fantastic news last night, so I'm on cloud nine." Ananda gushed.

"That's great, would you care to share?"

Ananda's smile widened, "Nope."

Hunter chuckled, "Well in that case, let's handle business first." He pointed to the papers on his desk.

Ananda took a seat in one of the chairs in front of his desk and read over the papers that he had presented.

"Colgate would like to extend your contract for another year. They have received wonderful feedback from your ads and want to book you for more."

Ananda shook her hands from side to side in celebration. "Awesome!"

"I negotiated with them back and forth for a while, but they are willing to give you 2.3 million dollars for this new campaign."

Ananda's mouth dropped open, "Are you for real right now?"

Hunter smiled, "Yes. And that's just the first deal. I also have an offer on the table from Zac Posen himself requesting you for his fashion show. Since he is requesting you personally for all of his runway shows as well as his print modeling he has agreed to pay you one million for the first year with your contract up for renegotiation at the end of the year."

Ananda's smile grew from ear to ear. She had no idea that she would be in this sort of demand after from just one Colgate commercial.

"This is craziness. Just a year ago, I was scraping by to pay my rent. Now I can afford to pay cash for my house! This is pure craziness!" Ananda jumped up to hug Hunter, "Oh thank you so much for everything that you have done for me. It's all because of you. All of it!" She beamed. "I'm so excited! Wait till I tell my Mama!"

Hunter laughed out loud "You arc very welcome, beautiful. I'm glad to be able to serve you anytime. Any good business for you is great business for my company."

"Yes indeed it is." Ananda agreed practically skipping around the room. "When do I begin work?"

"Zac's next show is two months away and he isn't scheduled to start his photo shoots for about four months so you have some time on those contracts, but Colgate would like to get you into the studio as soon as next week."

"Great!"

"You'll be here in New York a lot the following months, so you may want to look for somewhere you can stay locally, or you can always stay at my loft with me." Hunter offered.

Ananda pondered his offer momentarily, "Thank you, but I need my own space. I'm used to living alone and doing my own thing." She told him.

"Fair enough, but the offer will continue to stand."

"Thank you Hunter." She smiled giving him a peck on the cheek before signing her Hancock to the contracts, "I appreciate you so much. Now I must be off, I have things to do, like shop before I head back home." She told him with a grin. "Life is just fabulous isn't it?" She said as she exited the door.

It absolutely is. Hunter said into his now lifeless office.

Lorna had been standing by Hunter's shut door waiting for Ananda to leave. As soon as she waltzed out past Lorna, Lorna practically ran into Hunter's office slamming the door behind her.

Hunter eyed Lorna as if she had lost her mind.

"Are you crazy?" He snapped at her, "You know better than to slam my office door that way. What is wrong with you?"

"Everything is wrong." A hysterical Lorna shouted at him, "I don't understand you. I have been working for you for years, I know you in and out. How you take your coffee with to teaspoons of sugar and three tablespoons of cream, how you like your corn beef on rye lightly toasted with a dash of honey mustard and a pickle on the side. You like you suits ironed with no crease, no starch on your shirt, no ice in your water, but ice in your tea. You hate wearing hats because it bothers the scar you have on the base of your hairline from when you fell and banged your head when you were little and needed twenty stitches. I know you like your woman to taste like strawberries and your dick sucked with an ice cube and you have the nerve to sit there and flaunt another woman in front of me? A woman who just so happens to work for you, just as I do? But only in a different capacity, Mister Don't Mix Business With Pleasure," she screamed bitterly.

Lorna continued shouting. "Well screw you and this job and Ananda. I will suffer no more of this indignity; you can take this job and shove it up your selfish black ass. I quit! You will never find anyone else to cater to you like I do. I worked night and day at your side as you built this little empire, and this is the thanks I get?" Lorna said as she flung his office door open and banged it off the wall then she stormed out where her coworkers were gawking at her wondering what happened.

Hunter sat back in his chair mesmerized by her performance. He hated to admit it but Lorna's sassiness had turned him on. Momentarily forgetting about Ananda he wondered where this spitfire personality of Lorna's had been for the past years she had worked for him. That was a side of her personality that he had never seen before and definitely hoped that he would see again. He respected anyone willing to take a stand and not be used as a floor mat and Lorna had just earned his respect. He would give her a few days to cool off then he would apologize with some flowers and tell her that she must come back to the office because he was destitute without her. He would say that she was right, he'd never be able to find another assistant like her who knew him so well, and, shaking his head with a sheepish grin, in so, so many ways.

Twenty-Three

"I don't know Tray. I'm tired. I may need to go to the doctor.

Lately I've been feeling really fatigued. I'm not sure if it's because I've been traveling between New York and home so much. I may need to slow down."

"How long has this been going on?" Tracey asked her concerned. She had come over to Ananda's house to pick her up to go shopping but Ananda looked as if she had been hit by a bus.

"The past two weeks or so. I must have picked up a bug somewhere. You know with all this commuting back and forth you tend to pick up peoples germs."

"Yeah, but nothing should be holding on to you for over two weeks time. Let me feel your forehead." Ananda sat up so Tracey could feel her head.

"Well you don't have a fever. When's the last time you had you period? You're not pregnant are you?"

"Pregnant?" Ananda echoed, "You know, that never crossed my mind." I hope that's not it. With the exception of being tired all the time I feel fine."

"Well feeling tired all the time isn't normal." Tracey ran her fingers through Ananda's short hair. "Tell me what you want me to do."

"Nothing. Go ahead and enjoy your day. It's not your fault that I'm feeling like a mess. Go shopping for me. See if you can find me something cute by Alexander McQueen."

Tracey laughed as she stood up, "Sick and still thinking about fashion. Girl you a trip. Are you sure you want me to leave?"

"Yes, I'm about to take a nap and there's no point in you sitting her to watch me sleep."

"True." Tracey leaned down and kissed her forehead, "If you need anything give me a holla and I'll bring it to you okay."

"Thank you boo." Ananda said as she curled back in her bed, closing her eyes as Tracey let herself out.

****

Oh my God! A wave of panic engulfed Ananda as she looked at the plus sign on the slender white stick and felt the room begin to spin. She finally had answers to her questions. The reason that she'd been so tired lately and why she had begun peeing as if she and the commode were BFF's.

There was no way that she could be pregnant; she didn't have the time for it. Hunter had her scheduled to be on the next flight to Milan to participate in Zac's runway show, as sick as she was feeling there was no way that she was going to be able to do that now. She was entirely too sick and would not be appearing in anyone's anything. Stomach churning made a beeline for the trashcan in the corner of her room since it was closer than the bathroom and heaved up what was left of her dinner from the previous night because she hadn't been able to force herself to eat anything today. After regurgitating all the contents of her stomach Ananda crawled, back to her bed and eased up on the side of it so that she could lie down.

Closing her eyes, she sighed in relief that she was now comfortably lying down. Her eyes had been closed for two second it felt like before she heard a soft creaking noise. Eyes popping open at the sound Ananda slowly sat up in her bed. Glancing around the room everything appeared normal and in place. She waited a full two minutes to see if she heard the noise again before laying her head back on the pillow satisfied that she'd heard nothing further. Letting her eyes drift closed again, she figured that it would be only a matter of minutes before exhaustion overcame her and shifted her back into a dreamland where she could relax.

Sensing that something was wrong Ananda woke up with a jolt. Smelling smoke her eyes snapped open and she had a weird feeling that she wasn't alone. As she tried to sit up she noticed that her body was restrained and she couldn't move. Not understanding what was happening or if she were still dreaming Ananda twisted her head to the side and her body froze.

Sitting in the chair Ananda kept in the corner of her room was Heather, Malcolm's wife smoking a cigarette and smiling.

"Hello Ananda."

Ananda's eyes narrowed as she stared at the woman sitting in her room as if she belonged there.

"What are you doing here?"

"I thought that you and I could chat so that we can come to an understanding about Malcolm." Heather told her as she calmly took a puff from her cigarette.

Ananda narrowed her eyes, "What is there to understand?"

"You seem to have a problem understanding what does and does not belong to you so I want to help you get it right." Heather pointedly informed her.

"The only thing I need to get right is when and where I'm going to fuck you up at. I won't be restrained forever and trust me you're going to regret this moment right here." Ananda warned her.

"Oh Ana, Ana." Heather sang as she stood and put her cigarette out on Ananda's nightstand, "That's what Tracey calls you right?" She laughed, "I'm not sure what I expected from you but I expected so much more. Usually Malcolm has better taste. I mean, I don't judge him for Merci because he was young and didn't know any better, but you are another story. He already had me when he met you so I'm not sure exactly what the attraction was."

"Don't kid yourself. You have a TV you've seen me on it. You know exactly why he keeps coming here and won't leave me alone. I have plenty of televisions and I've never seen you on one so you do the math." Ananda spat at Heather as her fingers kept moving under the covers. She always slept with a blade and now she thanked heaven that she did. Fingers finally able to grasp her blade made Ananda's day. Moving her hand back and forth, she cut through the restraints very slowly so that she didn't cause too much attention to herself as Heather continued with her verbal assault.

"You know what's sad you don't even realize how pathetic you sound. You are fooling with a married man, but that ends tonight. I'm done with this." Heather withdrew a blade and walked up to Ananda pressing it up to her throat. "I really don't want to harm you sweet Ana, please don't make me. You stay away from Malcolm you hear me?"

Ananda nodded slowly, "I do hear you, but you didn't understand *me*!" She told Heather bringing her fist down hard in the center of Heather's throat causing Heather to let go of the knife she was holding and gasp for air. Quickly scrambling to her feet Ananda grabbed a hold of the knife and threw it as far as she could out her bedroom door then turned her attention back on Heather.

Seeing the rage in Ananda's eyes Heather tried to suck air into her lungs as well as keep Ananda at a distance.

"You picked the wrong one to play these games with. Ananda yelled as she dived across her bed and landed on top of Heather and striking her with punch after punch until her hand hurt and Heather's face was beaten to a bloody pulp.

Picking up the phone Ananda dialed 911 letting them know Heather had broken into her house and that she'd beaten her up pretty badly and she needed an ambulance. Hanging up with the dispatcher, she immediately phoned Malcolm to let him know what happened. Once she told Malcolm, what was going on she hung up and ran to the bathroom where she threw up in the commode. Dry heaving was more like it because she didn't have any food in her system. Feeling woozy herself Ananda passed out on the bathroom floor until the police and the ambulance arrived for her and Heather.

Twenty-Four

*M*alcolm felt like a man gone mad as he visited first Heather's hospital room and then Ananda's. Ananda was awake just a little groggy.

"Hey. How are you feeling?" He asked pulling the hospital chair closer to her bed."

Ananda attempted a half smile. "I'm doing alright. Still a little queasy but nothing I can't handle. I'm just highly irritated that your wife called herself breaking into my place, tying me up and trying to threaten me at knifepoint. Is she crazy?" Ananda was no longer upset, she was thankful to be lying down being taken care of by the nurses and doctors.

"Here you are! Oh my god what happened?" Tracey barged in the room ignoring Malcolm while she went to the bed to hug Ananda.

Ananda told her the story and Tracey was shocked. "You have got to be kidding me. I would never think that Heather was capable of something like that, but you know men make women crazy-and judging by the fact that her husband is here in your room and not hers it would appear that you didn't heed my advice."

"You don't have to talk about me like I'm not sitting her Tracey." Malcolm interrupted.

Tracey spun to look at him, "If I had something to say to you then I would, but as it stands I have absolutely nothing to say to someone as simple minded as you are. You are the cause for all this drama and you don't seem to care."

Malcolm stood, "Of course I care and that's why I took the first flight that I could to get here to check on them."

"You're a piece of work and I can't stand to be around you." Tracey turned back to face Ananda and placed a kiss on her cheek. "You get better hun. I'm a go and see about Heather. Someone in this room has to look out for her and obviously it ain't gonna be her husband." Tracey huffed before she left the room with an attitude.

Ananda leaned her head back on the pillows and closed her eyes. Her body was so far past exhaustion she didn't know how to describe how she was feeling at this point.

"You're not going to press charges are you?" Malcolm asked her.

"That is up to the police. They know that she broke in and tied me up and that I had to fight her off, so I'm not sure what is going to happen now."

"Heather is going through a lot right now. She doesn't mean any harm."

That statement forced Ananda to open her eyes abruptly. "What do you mean she didn't mean any harm? She tied me up and held a knife to my neck." Ananda snapped, "Do you think that she was playing? Because I do not, I took her as a threat and beat her as such. I'm from the streets and that type of action writes you a death wish."

"I know bu--" Malcolm began.

"You know what, get out of here." Ananda yelled. "I don't have time for this, go back to your wife, that's where you need and want to be anyway."

"It's not like that, it's just that she had just received the separation papers and was consumed by emotion."

"I could give two flying shits what she was consumed with. Do I look like I care?"Ananda shouted back at him. "Do you know what I am consumed with? Huh? I just found out that I was pregnant, today. The same day your wife chooses to attack me. I don't have time for this right this second okay. Now leave!"

"You're pregnant?" Malcolm whispered dumbfounded. "Is it mine? I'm not sure if I can be pregnant right now. I'm trying to get my stuff together and get out this whole situation with Heather and make sure my girls are okay."

"Seriously if you don't leave and I mean right now I will call security to get you out of her. You are so selfish, like I care if you can or cannot be pregnant right now. News flash ding dong I'm the pregnant one and it has nothing to do with you, whether you're the father or not it is all my decision and what I want to do thank you very much."

Ananda held down the button for the nurse's station. "Yes." A pleasant voice came across the speaker, "Can you please send security to room 207. I have someone in my room that refuses to leave." Ananda told the nice nurse. "Of course, I'll send someone right down." "Thank you so much." Ananda said releasing the call button.

"Did you really call hospital security on me?"

"I absolutely did and they are on their way so you should get out. I'm tired of being nice to you. Leave me alone."

"Fine." Malcolm said as he spun on his heel and exited the room.

Entering Heather's room again, hoping that she was now awake, Malcolm felt sorry for her with her face completely bandaged looking like a sight for sore eyes. Tracey was also in the room sitting next to Heather's bed holding her hand in hers.

"Must you really keep following me?" Tracey spat out.

"I'm trying to check on Heather. I don't care what you do." Malcolm told her.

"You're the reason for this whole mess. Now both of my friends are in the hospital. What kind of man are you?" Tracey asked disgustedly. She was not a fan a Malcolm. He was as doggish as they come and the bad part is he didn't think he was a dog, he honestly thought that he was a nice guy and she was just the one to break that misconception.

She decided to answer her own question. "You are nothing more than a trifling, selfish boy operating under the insane delusion that you're such a nice guy when obviously you're not. Both of these women would be so much better off without you and the sooner they realize it, the sooner they'll have a much better life."

"Are you finished?" Malcolm asked her calmly, not in the mood to deal with a rant from someone he was barely acquainted with.

"You'll know when I am done." Tracey pulled her hand out of Heather's and stood up, "I can't stand to be in your presence." She said as she brushed shoulders hard with Malcolm and then left the room.

Malcolm breathed a sigh of relief that she was gone. Making his way to the chair she had just vacated he sat next to Heather and picked up her hand.

"How are you feeling?" He asked her when he noticed that her eyes were slanted open.

"Hurt." She responded. He could tell she was hurt, if the swelling around her eyes was any indication of what her face looked like under the bandages.

"What happened?" Malcolm asked her.

"That hoe attacked me." Heather spoke in a raspy whisper. "I went to her place to get her to understand some things and she just attacked me for no reason."

"The police report says you broke in and tied her up." Malcolm said looking at her for an explanation, "You do know that it is illegal to break into someone's place and tie them up holding them hostage in their own space."

A single tear slid down Heather's face. "I just want her to leave you alone." Her fingers squeezed his, "Why can't you leave her alone. I thought you loved me."

"I do love you, but I love her too." Malcolm felt that it was time to come clean. "I never meant for anything like this to happen."

"What exactly did you mean to happen? First Merci kills herself then your girlfriend and your wife end up in the hospital from a fight. What did you expect to happen, Malcolm? Please tell me what you expected. You know something? I don't care." Heather said feeling more agitated by the moment, slowly working herself up into a fit. "Just leave me alone. I don't want you here right now." She said after forcing herself to calm down.

Malcolm released her hand and stood. "I'll be back." He promised her as he leaned down kissing her forehead before exiting the room.

****

Hunter entered Ananda's hospital room with flowers after hearing about the ordeal that she experienced.

"Hey beautiful."

Ananda gratefully smiled when she heard Hunter's voice. "Hi."

He came to the bed and kissed her cheek before placing the flowers on the vent by the wall then unbuttoned his suit jacket before sitting in the chair by her bed.

"What did you do to get yourself cooped up in the hospital?"

"I'm a little pregnant and got into a big fight." Ananda laughed, "The combination resulted in me lying right here in this hospital bed."

Hunter's body stiffened when he heard the word pregnant. "You're pregnant? Are you sure?"

"Yes, I'm sure."

"Is it mine?" Hunter asked her right away.

Ananda took a few moments to herself before answering, "There is a fifty percent chance." She told him honestly.

"When can we find out?"

"It's too early right now. I just found out that I was pregnant today." She told him.

"This is a bad time for you to be pregnant business wise." Hunter reminded her.

"I didn't forget about business, but I'm pregnant now so what do you want me to do?"

"You still have options since it's so early."

Ananda stared at Hunter as if he had lost his mind. "If you're implying what I think that you're implying then an option has been chosen and a decision has been made. I'm keeping my baby." Ananda told him with finality in her voice. "Business wise I can do as many photo shoots as you can book up until I begin to show, but runway is out. I've been so sick that I can't possibly walk in a show right now. See if you can renegotiate the deal with Zac for me to do print ads now and runway after I have the baby."

Hunter sighed in frustration, "I'll see what I can do. But this makes the company look bad. I just got you that deal and here you go getting yourself pregnant."

"In all fairness, it has been about two months since you got me the deal and last I checked I couldn't get pregnant alone. Someone had to assist with that."

"Someone is right and you don't even know who the someone is." Shaking his head Hunter stood, "At this time I will have to end any further encounters with you that are not business related. I will call you about the contract renegotiation. Please let me know when the baby is born so that my paternity can be established – or", clearing his throat, "excluded. Keep in touch with me and if you need anything don't hesitate to call me." He turned and left the hospital room without looking back.

Ananda shook her head, she had told both men that she was pregnant and both had an issue with it. She was fine with it though, thanks to her lucrative modeling contracts she was more than capable of taking care of her baby herself. She didn't need either of them.

Ananda smiled as Tracey reentered her room.

"How do you feel about the title Godmommy?" Ananda asked Tracey.

"Godmommy huh? Why would that be my title?"

"Because I'm pregnant and I want you to be my baby's Godmother." Ananda told her.

"You're pregnant." Tracey sat down next to her, "Are you sure?"

"Yup, very sure. Please be excited." Ananda said desperately, "I told Malcolm and Hunter and neither of them are excited, I think they both want me to get rid of it."

"You don't think that would be the good thing to do? And I'm assuming that since you told both men that you don't know who the father is."

"Tracey, are you serious right now? You want me to abort my baby?"

"No, that's not what I said."

"That's what it sounded like to me."

"You just shouldn't bring this baby into your mess. This whole Malcolm thing is out of control and he is Heather's husband. You seem to keep forgetting that."

"I never forget because you won't allow me to. What if it's Hunter's? You're so stuck on that Malcolm tip that you not considering anything else."

"You just said neither man seems to be interested in a baby at the moment. Just get rid of it no one will know."

"I would know and I want my baby regardless of either man's interests or intentions." Ananda didn't recognize this callous cold Tracey and wondered what had happened to her "ride or die" friend.

"I just think it's a bad idea. Do you ever stop to think about Heather in all of this?"

"What is the deal with you being on some kind of Heather kick? Y'all back to being friends or something."

"More or less. We never really stopped being friends we just lost touch with one another."

"Just so I have this right, you're okay being friends with the woman that broke into the apartment of your friend since kindergarten, who is closer than a sister to you? She held me at knife point! I'm just trying to be clear here as to what is being said. Am I to understand that all of that is okay with you?" Ananda is struggling to believe her ears.

"I mean come on!" Tracey raised her voice slightly, " You act as if you weren't sleeping with her husband Ananda. You may still be sleeping with him, we don't know. You're lucky she didn't kill you because I know that I damn sure would have or at the very least tried. You know how I feel about this topic. You are wrong and you know it. I'm not sugar coating anything for you. I know we're friends, but wrong is wrong and I'm not going to go along with you for the ride on this one like everything is all well and good because it is not."

"Well aren't you calling the kettle black." Ananda began,

"Let me stop you before you go any farther and say something that you will regret."

"I never regret anything I say Tracey and you know it. If I say it I mean it. All of a sudden, you walking around all holier than thou like you didn't use to work the streets, or pole or whatever you were doing. You act like you being a high-class prostitute for celebrities somehow isn't as bad as being a low class one. Trust me it's all the same." Ananda told her snidely.

"You know what I don't need is you over there judging me by my past. You bring that stuff up every time I don't agree with something that you're doing. My life has completely changed I no longer live my life that way, but just for the record, I'm not ashamed of it or regret it. It is my past and that is where it will stay. Cameron is the best thing that came out of that time in my life and I won't have you lay there trying to make me feel cheap and used."

"I'm not trying to make you feel cheap or used. I just want you to stop judging me."

"You know what," Tracey gave an irritated sigh, "All we're doing is talking in circles. We've been doing this the last few months and our friendship is suffering because of it, so let's do this instead," Tracey hesitated, "Until you get your life together and stop sleeping with married men I can no longer associate with you. Our friendship is on pause indefinitely. Get yourself together and then maybe we can begin to rebuild from there. Until you get to that place however, I have nothing else to say to you." Tracey told her walking out the room.

Ananda stared at the door Tracey had just exited and was shell-shocked unable to believe that Tracey had actually ended their almost three-decade friendship in a matter of seconds.

Twenty-Five

*N*othing has changed. He still yearns for her. Months later,

he still calls her and thinks I don't know. I see the way he stares at her photo in his phone. The look in his eyes says everything that needs to be said. His heart, where it once almost belonged to me solely belongs to her now. I can understand that. Hard to accept, but I can understand it. Unfortunately, for them both, he belongs to me and I won't be without him. There is no life for me without him in it. He is my life and since he won't be a part of my life, I'll remove him from his.

Twenty-Six

$\mathcal{S}$itting in the hospital room for the third day staring at her bundles of joy Ananda couldn't believe that eight months had gone by so quickly and she was now the mother to a bouncing boy and girl that were born seven weeks early but doing just fine. This had been the longest and loneliest eight months of her life. Everyone close to her had pulled a disappearing act.

Ananda was stalling on opening the envelope she'd received the day before containing the paternity results of the twins that she kept sitting on the bed with her. Both Malcolm and Hunter had willingly surrendered their DNA a few days ago wanting to know the results.

Satisfied that her tiny bundles were sleeping peacefully in their little cart beds as Ananda liked to call them, she reached for the envelope and opened it.

She sucked in a breath of shocked air when she read the results not certain that something like this could be possible. Both men were the fathers. Hunter was the father of her daughter Ariane and Malcolm was the father of her son Maddox. She couldn't believe that the twins had different fathers, in what world did something like this happen she wondered.

Later that day, Ananda groaned as she picked up her cell to text her assistant Tiffany that had gone to the cafeteria to bring her some lunch. Quickly typing the text and setting the phone back down. Ananda glanced up when there was a knock at her door.

"Come in." She called out.

Malcolm entered.

"What are you doing here?" Ananda asked him. She had spoken to Malcolm off and on during her pregnancy but hadn't seen him since the last time that she'd been hospitalized after the fight with his wife.

"I came to see you and the babies." Malcolm could see the hurt and anger in her eyes, "I've missed you," he whispered.

Ananda said nothing and pointed at the infants on the left side of her bed sleeping.

"They're beautiful." Malcolm gushed as he walked over to gaze at the babies. "Did you get the results back from the DNA test yet?"

"Sure did." Ananda told him in an indifferent tone.

Malcolm looked up from the babies wondering why Ananda was taking her time in telling him if her were the father or not. "Well?"

"Congratulations, you have a son. Maddox is yours."

"I don't understand, how is one mine and not the other?" Malcolm considered himself relatively smart but this he couldn't comprehend.

"Yeah," Ananda began sensing his confusion, "I didn't quite understand it either, but the nurse came in and explained it to me. Basically it's called heteropaternal superfecundation, which is when two eggs from the same mother get fertilized by two different fathers within the same ovulation period."

"Wow." Malcolm replied, "That's crazy."

"That's what I was thinking. Studies show that it happens in every one of four hundred sets of twins, so I would be the one huh?" Ananda tried to pass off a giggle to lighten the mood, but nothing about it was funny.

"Are you doing okay?" Malcolm asked as he came back over to her bed.

"I'm as well as can be expected." Ananda told him.

"I've missed you," he said again.

"Really? You have a funny way of showing it." Ananda told him. "Where have you been for the last eight months, I know you called but you couldn't take one second to fly out here and see me? Not one?"

"I was busy trying to sort out my life. When Heather received the separation papers all hell broke loose."

"Right, Heather. How is that situation by the way?"

"I retracted the separation papers."

Ananda snorted, "Big surprise there."

"I felt bad. After the fight that put her in the hospital, there's no way that I could walk out on her too. I just couldn't do it. It doesn't mean that I love you any less."

Tracey's words came back to haunt Ananda *There's nothing you can do that will make him leave his wi*fe she'd said. Ananda was now inclined to agree.

"You don't have to explain. Go home to your wife. You can visit your son whenever you want I won't keep you from him, but crazy Heather can't be around him. She's too gone in the head, no telling what she'll do to my baby if she's alone with him. So you'll have to come here to see him."

"That won't be a problem at all. Thank you." He told her, "And now that some time has passed I can submit the separation papers again."

"Please don't, I don't need the drama in my life. My main concern is my children's safety at this point, It's no longer all about me,"

"It'll be all about us. I'll move up here and everything. It'll be you and me."

"Seeing is believing, Malcolm, until I see a change I can't believe a word that you say." Ananda told him just as Tiffany came rushing into the room.

Tiffany had been a godsend. She doubled up as assistant and publicist when needed. The agency had given Ananda Tiffany once her load picked up and they had found out that she was pregnant. During the past eight months when she was virtually alone with only her mother on her side, Tiffany had been the one making the midnight runs when she was craving food and rubbing her feet when she had been standing all day. Hunter had been able to find her some pregnancy modeling gigs, so she had worked up until the baby came. He may not have communicated with her personally, but professionally he'd kept her schedule completely filled with print ad opportunities and on the business end, she was very grateful.

"I received your text, what's going on? Are you okay?" Tiffany asked taking out a pad and paper.

"Yes, I just need you to do damage control before the media finds out about the twins' paternity." With Ananda's newfound celebrity, she knew the paternity of the twins was going to be a runaway train once the tabloids got a hold of it. "I want you to set up a press conference and make an announcement about what is going on and that at this time we expect and hope that everyone will respect our privacy."

Tiffany jotted all the information down. "No problem I will get right on this and have the press release ready for your review by noon."

"You're amazing. Thank you." Ananda praised her as she lay down on the hospital pillows, "Can you hand me my phone before you leave? I guess I should let Hunter know before it becomes public knowledge." Tiffany handed Ananda her cell phone and Ananda immediately dialed Hunter's office.

"Mr. Lewis' office." Ananda rolled her eyes at the ceiling when she heard Lorna's voice on the other end.

"Hello Lorna, may I speak to Hunter please."

"May I ask who is calling please?"

"Lorna, would you stop playing games, okay? You know this is Ananda and you have caller ID. Put Hunter on the phone," Ananda said tersely. Classical music came across the line and Ananda realized that she had been placed on hold without warning.

Rude bitch she thought to herself.

"This is Hunter."

"Hi Hunter, it's me."

"Ananda?"

"Yes."

"Long time no hear, how have you been? How are the babies?"

'Everyone is wonderful. I don't want to hold you up, I just want you to that the paternity results did come back, you are the father of a daughter her name is Ariane and that Tiffany is about to do a press conference announcing the results of the paternity test because the twins have different fathers. This is a courtesy call just so that you are aware before the media finds out."

Hunter shook his head as he sat at his desk. Thinking how he managed to get himself caught up in what he sure was going to be the scandal of the year. Of all the women to be the mother of his child, he picks the hoe that manages to have twins with different fathers. She was a beautiful hoe, but a hoe nevertheless. His colleagues were going to have a field day with this one.

Hunter cleared his throat, "When can I come down to see her?"

"Come down whenever you'd like. I'll be leaving the hospital tomorrow, so you can come by my place to visit with her.

"Great. I'll give you a call when I'm on my way down and congratulations." He said coolly

"Thanks" Ananda responded in the same manner as she hung up the phone.

Twenty-Seven

After the embarrassment of the whole ordeal with Ananda and the paternity of the twins, Hunter made it a point to no longer have anything to do with her. He'd take care of his daughter but that was all. Today was the first day that he was going down to Maryland to visit with his daughter who was now three months. He was glad that Ananda had called to give him a heads up about the press conference shortly after the babies' birth because as soon as it went viral his phone rang nonstop. He resented that Ananda had made him like one of the common folk from the Maury Show and just couldn't bring himself to make the trip to see them before now.

Hunter had rented a car and he and Lorna pulled up to Ananda's new home that she moved into not too long after she'd brought the twins home. Making their way to the front door Hunter rang the doorbell.

Ananda was expecting Hunter to visit, he'd phoned that morning to say that he was on his way, when she opened the door she hadn't expected to see Lorna there as well.

"Hello." She stepped back allowing the duo to enter. "Hunter it is so nice to see you, Lorna this is a surprise."

"Nice to see you again Ananda." Lorna icily responded.

"Hunter you can come up to the nursery." Ananda told him. As Lorna made an attempt to follow Ananda stopped her short, I'm sorry Lorna only family is allowed in the twins' nursery, but you are more than welcome to have a seat in the family room."

"Oh." Lorna spoke clearly annoyed, "I thought everyone was family considering how you get around."

Ananda bit her tongue for only a moment, "You can leave." She turned back to Hunter "Sorry Hunter but I don't like garbage in my home. You'll have to return her to your car."

Hunter shook his head as he escorted Lorna back to the car. "You couldn't be quiet for two minutes. This isn't about you." He scolded her, "I'm here to see my daughter. You'll wait here till I return." He told her as he unlocked the car for her to get inside. "I'll be back shortly."

Ananda was waiting when Hunter came back into the house. "Follow me." She guided him up the spiral staircase and down the hall to the twins' nursery where Malcolm was sitting in the rocking chair holding a sleeping Maddox.

"Malcolm. Congratulations." Hunter said as he nodded at the man.

"Likewise." Malcolm responded.

Hunter approached the crib that his daughter was lying in and marveled at how tiny she was. He looked over at Ananda, "Is it okay if I hold her?"

Ananda smiled, "Of course it is, she's your daughter." Ananda reached into the crib and picked up Ariane so that she could hand her to Hunter, you can sit in the other rocking chair if you like. Hunter walked over to the chair staring into his baby girl's eyes the entire time, upset with himself for waiting three months to see her.

Sensing his amazement, Ananda says, "I know, she's beautiful right?"

Hunter nodded, "She looks just like you. She's going to be gorgeous."

"She's already gorgeous," Ananda gazed at Ariane with love in her eyes. "I can't wait to see the amazing things she's going to do and the person that she is will become. The same with Maddox, they are my little miracles." Ananda replied.

"They are amazing." Malcolm chimed in.

"Yes they are." Hunter agreed.

Ananda quietly left the room as the fathers held their infants to retrieve a camera. Tiptoeing back into the room to not disturb either one with their offspring Ananda took a panoramic photo for the priceless moment that she was observing and wanted to remember forever.

Twenty-Eight

$\mathcal{T}$he twins were celebrating their first birthday with a huge
backyard barbeque at home. Ananda couldn't believe how fast
time had gone by. Ariane and Maddox were her life now. She
lived and breathed for them. Only taking modeling jobs that didn't
require she be away from her babies for extended periods of time.
As their mother, she felt that she should be the one around to take
care of her own children. Even Malcolm had kept true to his word
by filing the separation papers and bringing himself and his two
girls to live with her and the twins.

While modeling had been great for her bank account, it came
with its shortcomings. She was once a fan of tabloids, but after
seeing your face plastered on more than a few covers with half-
truths and outright lies as the headlines you learn to resent them.

When her babies were born, the tabloids had a field day with
the knowledge of their split paternity. Having a press conference

to break the news herself hadn't helped contain the media circus and the backlash had been horrible. Ananda had been called every name in the book except a child of God, but somehow miraculously she remained one of the most sought after models in the industry and she relished in that. Talent is wonderful, but notoriety is golden, the Kardashians got it right.

Smiling as she watched her two bundles of energy wobble around the yard, her face registered shock when she saw Tracey enter through the back gate. The same Tracey she hadn't seen or heard from since the first day she'd found out that she was pregnant.

Tracey sheepishly made her way toward Ananda. "Hey boo." She said opening her arms as if she expected Ananda to step into them and grant her a hug."

"What are you doing here?" Ananda asked her with no cut cards, not having many words for Tracey today.

"I came to the party so that I could see my godchildren."

"You're what?" Ananda laughed, "Tracey, are you delusional? My babies are not your godchildren."

Tracey look genuinely confused, "What do you mean? I specifically remember you asking me to be the Godmother."

"You're right, I did and I specifically remember you walking out of my hospital room saying we were no longer friends, as if we were still in kindergarten or something." Ananda stared at her, "I meant that is how it went, please correct me if I'm saying something that isn't true here."

"No, what you're saying is accurate." Tracey nodded.

"Alright, at least we agree on one thing. Now, back to my original question, why are you here? You weren't invited."

Tracey's peppy smile collapsed under the weight of Ananda's words, "Come on Ana, I miss you alright. I miss my friend. I apologize for being such a jerk and more importantly for not being there when you needed me through you pregnancy. Can you forgive me?"

"No, I cannot. You hurt me. You were supposed to be my girl you left me hanging like we don't go back to hopscotch and freeze tag."

"What I did was wrong. I was being very judgmental and while I still don't agree with the choices that you made I didn't have to stop being your friend because of it."

"I'm glad that you realized that." Ananda said as she took off running to catch Maddox before he toppled over into the grass. Tracey ran behind her.

"Do you forgive me now?" Tracey looked at the ground giving Ananda pleading puppy dog eyes.

Ananda laughed, "Will that make you stop following me around like a lost dog?"

Tracey nodded. "Okay," Ananda told her, "But if you do anything like that again you cancel the puppy eyes and the begging and all that because I'm not going to want to hear it."

"I come in peace." Tracey bowed down, "Now who is this?" Tracey asked sitting on the ground next to Ananda.

"This is Maddox." Ananda turned him to face Tracey, "Maddy this is Ms. Tracey." Maddox was all smiles when he looked at Tracey displaying his two front teeth that had recently come in.

"Well aren't you handsome Maddy." Tracey smiled back at him. Ananda was surprised when he reached his hands out for Tracey to pick him up.

"Wow, he must like you." She said as Tracey took Maddox out her arms, "He never goes to anyone."

"He knows his Godmommy when he sees her."

"The jury is still out on that Godmommy bit. You've only been back in the picture five minutes. I'll keep you posted on when they return with a verdict."

"Oh come on Ana. Look how cute they are, let me be their godmother."

Ananda was unmoved, "They've been cute for a year now. Where have you been? A godmother would have been there. Excuse me for a moment." She told Tracey leaving Maddox with her as she checked to see where Ariane had wondered off too because she couldn't see her anywhere.

"Ma, have you seen Ariane?" Ananda said coming up behind her mother.

"She's right here honey, I have her." Her mother turned around and Ariane was asleep in her arms. "Oh thank goodness I was beginning to worry." Ananda let out a sigh.

"Yeah, some strange lady was lurking in her space for too long, it made me nervous so I went and got my grandbaby."

"What strange lady?" Ananda's body instantly became alert.

Her mother pointed by the gate, "She was standing by the gate; I'm not sure where she went. Something strange about her though. I didn't get a good vibe. I think she came with Tracey."

Ananda's heart leapt into her throat as she whipped around to where she'd left Tracey sitting holding Maddox and realized Tracey was gone.

"Where is Tracey?"

"I'm not sure." Her mother answered, I haven't seen her since she came into the yard.

Ananda began to panic as she frantically took to running around the yard yelling Maddox's name.

Malcolm and Hunter ran up to her, "What's wrong?" They asked in unison.

Ananda whole body began to shake, "Have either of you seen Tracey?"

Both looked confused, "I thought you and Tracey weren't friends anymore."

Tears began pouring down Ananda's face, "We're not. She was here in this spot holding Maddox when I went to check on Ariane."

Hunter studied the worry on Ananda's face, "Are you sure? No one has seen her."

"Yes," She screamed, "Yes, I'm sure! My mother saw her when she came in too. I'm going to check the house."

"Maddy!" Ananda yelled as she entered the house through the sliding doors in the back and began opening all the doors in the house while continuing to scream Maddox's name until she had checked every room in the house.

"He's gone. My baby is gone!" Ananda whimpered running back outside the house and losing her mind in the process. "She took my baby! Find her please!" Ananda slid to the ground in hysterics. "Find my baby!"

The commotion in the backyard had caused Ariane to wake up wailing. Hearing Ariane, Ananda jumped up and went to her mother removing Ariane out of her hands as she rocked her daughter trying to comfort her tears as hers raced on.

Twenty-Nine

"It's been three months, what do you want to do?" Malcolm asked.

Ananda shook her head as she rocked back and forth in the nursery that the twins had once shared. Maddox still hadn't been returned home and no amount of money, police force, FBI, no one seemed to be able to find her baby, Tracey or Heather. This was payback. Ananda kept saying to herself. She had barely managed to live with the guilt she carried for killing Merci so many years ago, but she had repented about that since having children of her own. But karma is real and it came back with a cruel, twisted vengeance and taken her beloved Maddy.

Ananda knew Malcolm wanted her to pack his things up so she didn't see them every day and continue to depress herself, but she couldn't do it. She couldn't pack her baby's belongings and act as if he didn't exist. She wasn't giving up hope. Her little angel was going to come home. He had too.

"It's my fault." Ananda kept rocking back and forth in the chair, "It's my fault. I walked away from him. I left him with Tracey. Even after all those months of not talking to her I took her at her word."

Malcolm knelt in front of Ananda as she kept rocking back and forth with eyes unseeing.

"You can't beat yourself up like this. You didn't know what was going to happen. There is no way that you could have known that Tracey was capable of something like this. You have to stop blaming yourself. Ariane, Caprice and Tatiana need a mother. I know you're hurting about Maddy, but you can't let the three girls suffer because you're feeling guilty, you have to keep living life for them, they don't understand any of this and why you don't talk to them anymore. When's the last time you held Ariane? Or looked at her for that matter?"

Ananda closed her eyes as the river of tears flooded her face. "I don't know how to be their mother now. I think about Maddy all the time. I don't know how to move on. I don't see how you can manage it either."

"You didn't give me a choice. With you holed up in this room crying all day, I have to take care of the girls. Someone has to make sure Tatiana is getting to and from school and doing her homework. Someone has the make sure that Caprice is learning to tie her shoes and count to a hundred. And someone has to get Ariane potty trained and teach her ABC's. This is all the stuff you're missing." Malcolm took her hand into his.

"Ariane knows her ABC's?" Ananda whispered.

"Not all of them. She's up to K, but she's getting better." Malcolm gave her a little smile. Listen, I miss Maddy more than you can know, he" his voice cracking on his words, "is my son. but we have to focus on the one's that are here. If you want to leave the room the same, that's fine I won't bother you about it again, if you promise me you'll at least attempt to come out and rejoin your family. How about having dinner with us tonight? I'm sure that the girls would love to see you."

Ananda blinked rapidly trying to see Malcolm through the tears. "Okay." She said slowly. Malcolm stood and latched onto Ananda's arm to help her out the chair. Once she was standing up he guided her down the stairs to the kitchen for dinner where the girls were waiting.

****

"Hi Hunter." Ananda spoke into her cell phone. She had been avoiding Hunter's call making him communicate with Tiffany and Malcolm only.

"Nice to hear your voice and to know you're no longer ducking me."

"I'm sorry."

"I know you've been going through a lot, but I need to know if you can return to work. You know you're under contract with Zac and he's been very lenient about the contract you signed-- in light of recent events, but I think that he's beginning to get antsy and on top of everything else that's going on in your life, I would hate to see you get sued as well. You understand of course."

"Yes, I understand. When is the next show?"

"This weekend. There are two shows, one on Saturday and one on Sunday. You will need to participate in both because you will be the featured model. Can they count on you being there?"

"Yes, I will be there." Ananda told him.

"That's amazing news. Now on a personal note, how are you holding up?"

"I'm not." Ananda stated flatly.

"You know if there is anything you need you can just let me know right?"

"I need my baby Hunter. Do you know where he is? If not, there is nothing that you can do for me. I promise to be there Saturday, I have to go."

"Wait, before you hang up, can you bring Ariane with you this weekend? I would love to see her."

"Yes, I'll bring her with me." Ananda told him as she hung up the phone. Trying to figure out how she could possibly pull it together for a high fashion Zac Posen show this weekend in New York. Lord, help me maintain, she said to herself as went into her closet and began to pack for her and Ariane.

Thirty

*H*eather watched her while she sat there as the technician applied the finishing touches of her make-up. She observed the woman that seemed to have her husband's heart from the first moment he had laid eyes on her. She couldn't understand how Ananda was able to achieve something that she had spent years trying to bring into fruition. The sight of Ananda alone was enough to make Heather's heart weigh heavy. For the life of her, she couldn't understand Ananda's secret, what kind of magic potion had she concocted that made everything in her universe fall into place and destroy everyone else's world?

Heather glanced down as Maddox slept in her arms. It had been a trial trying to hide in the venue overnight with a toddler that seemed to want to make it his mission in life to be noisy. It was wonderful what a couple spoonfuls of Benadryl could do. Now he was sound asleep not causing any problems at all and she was grateful. The past couple of months on the run with a one year old had pushed her to the limit. She and Tracey had been all over the news, which had forced Tracey's husband Cameron into the limelight. Heather felt no remorse about Tracey's situation. Tracey was a little too gullible. It had been rather easy for Heather to reel her into her way of thinking because of the things that she and Tracey had endured together during their younger days and her own marital struggles with Cameron. Heather played off those emotions and Tracey had been putty in her hands.

It had been all too easy to make Tracey turn on Ananda, her home girl since the age of five. Ride or die be damned, that Tracey didn't know the meaning of true friendship. With all the media hype surrounding "basketball wife" Tracey, Heather had had to get rid of her. Anyway, she was starting to go soft on me. Good riddance, she thought. I hope that the fish got to whatever remained of her at the bottom of the ocean.

As Heather watched Ananda transform into a supermodel before her eyes, it hurt her to her heart to think this, but she actually respected Ananda in a way. She was a true go-getter and didn't have a problem fighting for what she felt was hers. In another life, Heather believed they could have been friends. But unfortunately, in this life they were sworn enemies, unknown to everyone but God, they had been born that way and that was the way they would die. Shifting Maddox in her arms, Heather waited patiently for her moment to show herself and what she was capable of doing for love.

****

Ananda was elated to be one of the featured models in New York's Fashion Week. This is just what the doctor ordered to take her mind off what was happening in her personal life. This had been a long time coming and she was thrilled. Hunter always made sure that she had the best of everything, including being in the best shows. She would be walking in Zac Posen's show and couldn't wait to strut her stuff on the runway. Smiling immediately when she saw Malcolm holding Caprice and Tatiana's hands, Tiffany and Hunter striding towards her through the massive dressing room with Hunter carrying a giggling Ariane in his arms, Ananda waited patiently for them to reach her.

"Hi Mama."

"Hi my little princess." Ananda responded pulling Ariane into her arms.

"Ana, you out did yourself. You look amazing and I just know this show is going to be fire!" Tiffany exclaimed.

"Thank you." Ananda said as she leaned in to give them all hugs saving Hunter for last. "Thank you for making all of this possible for me," she told him "I really appreciate it."

"You made it possible." Hunter whispered in her ear. "Thank you for taking me along for the ride."

"Okay, okay, enough of that sappy business talk, we've gotta get back to our seats." Tiffany interrupted laughing.

Ananda laughed loudly, "Yes ma'am" grudgingly handing Ariane back to Hunter. "Give mama a kiss please." Malcolm leaned over and Ananda playfully swatted his arm, "Not you! My little boo." She said leaning in giving Ariane a peck on the lips.

"Can't blame a brother for trying." Malcolm laughed.

"Yeah, yeah. Bye." Ananda smirked as she watched them walk back out to the front where their seats were located. Making her way to a quiet corner, Ananda closed her eyes to say a quick prayer before the show.

Malcolm deposited the girls and then reentered the back stage area amidst the hustle and bustle where Ananda was preparing to walk the runway. Finding her in the corner of the dressing area during her private moments as she looked to be in prayer, Malcolm thought that she resembled an angel. He stood patiently in front of her without making a sound waiting for her to complete her chat with the Lord.

Ananda said amen silently in her head and opened her eyes to find Malcolm staring at her with all the love in the world reflecting through his eyes. Ananda's breath caught as she stared at this man that had caused so much damage to her spirit and her heart, but had found a way to mend it too.

"You're not supposed to be here, the show is about to begin."

"I wanted to be here for you." Malcolm stated plainly without taking a step toward her and showing her that he had all the love in the world to give to her.

"Thank you I really appreciate that." Ananda told him, "Thank you for helping me to see that I needed to get up and try to live some type of life again. I would still be sitting in that rocking chair if it weren't for you."

"Showtime in five minutes. Start lining up please." The show director yelled to all the models.

"I have to go." Ananda stepped forward placing a soft kiss on Malcolm's lips.

Malcolm grabbed her up by the waist, "I love you, promise me you'll marry me."

Ananda glanced up at Malcolm, "You can't spring that on me right this minute, you're not even divor--" Halted mid-sentence by the sight of Heather over Malcolm's shoulder, in a wedding dress emerging from behind a wardrobe stand with a silver semi-automatic pistol balanced in her hand and little Maddox asleep in her arms.

"My baby!" Ananda whispered. Malcolm immediately spun around.

"What the --" Malcolm shouted making people look in their direction and then watching as panic set in and models began screaming and scrabbling to get out the way of the woman wielding the gun.

"I knew you would be here." Heather spoke to Malcolm and then paused, "With her." She snapped her head towards Ananda looking her up and down from head to toe. "I won't live without you Malcolm. Why can't you understand that!" Heather snapped as she repeatedly tapped the pistol against the side of her head.

Ananda knew if they didn't calm Heather down this would end badly. What was taking security so long? She thought to herself as she squinted her eyes a little trying to see if Maddox was okay, but he appeared to be fine and in a deep sleep. Sighing in relief she was grateful that her baby was still alive as she knew that he would be. A mother never gives up hope. Ever.

Ananda knew that she had to do something because she could tell that Heather was growing more and more desperate with each moment that passed and it would only be a matter of time before she lost her composure completely.

"Heather please listen and hear me, this is not what you think it is. I am done with Malcolm." Ananda lied attempting to step away from Malcolm who, in his shock of what was unfolding did not recognize the ruse. He would not let her out of his grasp thereby making the situation worse.

Heather studied Ananda with tears in her eyes, "I believe you. I really do, but I won't live without him and he can't live without you." She said sadly as if to her there was no other alternative to what she was about to do and this was her way of justifying what must be done. Aiming the gun at Ananda's head Heather's gun went off.

Malcolm stood in disbelief as Ananda slumped in his arms. He could tell without looking down at her that she was dead. Letting go of her lifeless body, he moved to lunge at Heather who was now aiming the weapon at him. He wasn't fast enough. Malcolm heard a sickening pop and then nothing as his body slammed head first to the floor.

"Ma'am halt right there!" Heather didn't bother to turn; she knew that the police had finally arrived.

Swiftly turning the gun to her head with tears sliding down her face Heather sat a sleeping Maddox on the floor, they would write about this in the future and say many terrible things about her, but they would never be able to say that she was a baby killer. That was taking it a step to far even for her. Without another thought Heather pulled the trigger and her world went black. A screaming Maddox awakened by the blasts of the gun crawled across the floor as he and the dress in which Heather had taken her vows with Malcolm, were splattered with her blood.

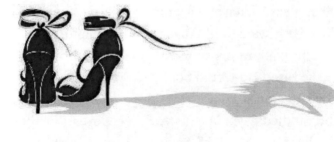

Epilogue

*H*unter sat on the bench near Ananda's grave holding tight to

Maddox and Ariane as each sat on his knees, little hands cuddling the teddy bears their mother had given them on their birthday with Caprice and Tatiana looking on. With a lump the size of a lemon in his throat, he fought back the only tears he had shed since Ananda's death. In less than three years he had made her into an international superstar and in a matter of seconds she had been taken from the industry, her son and daughter, and the world.

"Ready to go?" Lorna asked him softly as she walked up and gently took Maddox thus freeing him up to carry Ariane.

"Yeah there's nothing more we can do here." He said sadly as the six of them made their way to the waiting car and away from Ananda's final resting place.

About the Author

A native of the Metropolitan of Washington, DC, Mychea has had a dream to have her words shown in print since the age of since she was a child. She is the author of fiction novels My Boyfriend's Wife, He Loves Me, He Loves You Not 1 & 2, Coveted and Vengeance and Playwright of her stage play He Loves Me, He Loves You Not and Coveted. In her spare time, Mychea loves to draw, model, act and plan events. She is hard at work on her next novel and stage play.

He Loves Me, He Loves You Not 3
Coming Soon!

Email the author mycheawrites@yahoo.com
www.mychea.com

Good2Go Films Presents

To order books, please fill out the order form below:
To order films please go to www.good2gofilms.com

Name: _____

Address: _____

City: _____ State: _____ Zip Code: _____

Phone: _____

Email: _____

Method of Payment: ☐ Check ☐ VISA ☐ MASTERCARD

Credit Card#:

_____

Name as it appears on card:

_____

Signature: _____

Item Name	Price	Qty	Amount
He Loves Me, He Loves You Not - Mychea	$14.99		
He Loves Me, He Loves You Not 2 - Mychea	$14.99		
Married To Da Streets – Silk White	$14.99		
My Boyfriend's Wife - Mychea	$14.99		
Never Be The Same – Silk White	$14.99		
Stranded – Silk White	$14.99		
Slumped – Jason Brent	$14.99		
Tears of a Hustler - Silk White	$14.99		
Tears of a Hustler 2 - Silk White	$14.99		
Tears of a Hustler 3 - Silk White	$14.99		
Tears of a Hustler 4- Silk White	$14.99		
The Teflon Queen – Silk White	$14.99		
The Teflon Queen 2 – Silk White	$14.99		
The Teflon Queen – 3 – Silk White	$14.99		
Young Goonz – Reality Way	$14.99		
Subtotal:			
Tax:			
Shipping (Free) U.S. Media Mail:			
Total:			

Make Checks Payable To:
Good2Go Publishing
7311 W Glass Lane
Laveen, AZ 85339

CPSIA information can be obtained at www.ICGtesting.com
Printed in the USA
BVOW01s1603170114

341932BV00005B/6/P